The Cave Above Delphi

The Cave Above Delphi

BY SCOTT CORBETT

ILLUSTRATED BY GIOIA FIAMMENGHI

HOLT, RINEHART AND WINSTON

NEW YORK   CHICAGO   SAN FRANCISCO

The Cave Above Delphi

one

"Now, what's *he* up to?" Hay wondered to himself, as he watched the Greek boy.

The boy was sitting in the seat behind the driver, just in front of Hay and his sister, on the bus from Athens to Delphi. The bus was rumbling along a curving mountain road in a misty morning fog that came and went in patches, but mostly came.

"It looks as if we're driving right off into space," Mrs. Hobbs remarked with a shiver. The children's parents were in the seat behind them.

"I think Mr. Kazantzakis has every curve memorized. If he forgets one, we're done for," declared Professor Hobbs cheerfully.

They knew the driver was Aristotle Kazantzakis because he was identified by a metal nameplate posted in the bus. The plate was printed in Greek

characters, but Professor Hobbs could read and speak
modern Greek, and even the children already knew
the alphabet well enough to work out "APISTOTE-
ΛES KAZANTZAKIS," which was not much different from the way the name would look in Roman
letters.

Mr. Kazantzakis seemed to enjoy his work. At the
moment, he had laid his cap aside, his dark brown
driver's cap with its shiny black visor, and he was
singing along with a tune that was coming from the
radio loudspeaker in the front of the bus. Whenever
the driver felt like hearing a little music, he would
turn on the radio and noisy, tinkling *bouzouki* tunes
would fill the air.

Julia pressed her snub nose against the window.
"Don't worry, Mom, it's not so bad. Sometimes a
place clears away in the fog and then you can look
straight down into the valley," she reported with
great satisfaction.

"I'd rather not, thank you," her mother said
firmly.

"Now, Livia, you must pretend to be brave and
set a good example for the children, or they might
become frightened," said Professor Hobbs, who
loved to tease her.

"Ho! Those two frightened? Fat chance. My one
comfort is that I don't have to waste time pretending
to be brave for their sake. Your mother is a coward,
children, and she doesn't care who knows it."

They laughed at this comfortable confession, and
Julia went back to pressing her nose against the win-

dow, ready to report further terrifying glimpses down the sheer hillsides. Hay continued to watch the Greek boy in front of him.

The boy was sitting by the window. Next to him was a man with a big twirly mustache who knew the bus driver. The man had fallen asleep with an Athens newspaper on his lap. At least, it had been on his lap until the boy had slyly taken it. There was just enough space between the seats to allow Hay to see him do it. He had slipped out an inside page and returned the rest of the paper to the man's lap. Now he was carefully folding the sheet together into a long thin strip.

Hadrian Hobbs—Hay's first name was really Hadrian; he was named after his father's favorite Roman emperor—Hadrian Hobbs had the mind of a detective. He loved to speculate about people, trying to figure out who they were and what they were up to. Short and fat, with somewhat sleepy-looking eyes and a small, solemn mouth, Hay gave few outward signs of the lively, inquiring mind he happened to possess. New teachers who saw him sitting like a lump in the back row of a classroom on the first day of school were not impressed. They thought they were stuck with a real dunce who would have to be dragged through the year's work by his heels. They soon changed their minds.

Sitting like a lump in his seat as the bus swayed around curves, Hay systematically put together what he knew about the Greek boy. He knew his first name was Nicki, because he had heard him called that by a boy who had come to the bus station with him. Without understanding all they said, he could tell they went to school together somewhere in Athens, or near Athens. The reason he understood some of what they said was that occasionally they exchanged a few words in English—and very well, too, without much foreign accent at all. He was sure they were in high school.

Nicki was tall. Hay judged him to be at least two years older than himself. The Greek boy had a long, thin face that was handsome in a foxy way. His quick grin sparkled with a flash of strong white teeth. The way he had laughed and joked with his friend reminded Hay of Juggy Hopkins, who was the class cut-up at home.

Hay could not see everything Nicki did, but he could see enough of his movements to guess the rest. After Nicki had folded together several thicknesses of the news page into a long thin strip, he took out a pocket knife, cut off the rest of the sheet, and wadded it up. The wad went into his pocket.

What was Nicki going to do with a long thin strip of paper several layers thick? Hay went to work trying to guess. If he were Juggy Hopkins, what would he have in mind? But try as he might, Hay could not think of anything interesting a boy might do with a long thin strip of folded newspaper.

Nicki waited until Mr. Kazantzakis was busy with an unusually tight hairpin curve before he made his next move. Then he unhurriedly leaned forward in a natural way that would not attract the attention of the people across the aisle, who were busy talking anyway, and took Mr. Kazantzakis' cap from its low shelf.

The instant Nicki did that, Hay's small mouth twitched into a grin and quickly went solemn again. He knew now what Nicki was going to do.

In no time at all the cap was on the shelf again, and Nicki was lying back in his seat, pretending to be asleep.

Hay sat back, too. He clasped his hands together on his stomach and twiddled his thumbs contentedly, waiting to see what would happen next. He stared at Mr. Kazantzakis' dark, glistening hair, and was glad it was so bushy.

After a few more curves a town appeared ahead and a roadside sign in both Greek and Roman letters announced:

ΛΕΒΑΔΙΑ

LEVADIA

"*Souvlakia,*" announced Professor Hobbs. "Levadia is famous for its *souvlakia,* in case you'd care to have any, children."

"Good! I'm starved! I could eat a hundred sticks!" Julia was always hungry. She ate enormous amounts of food when it suited her, and remained thin as a rail. Poor Hay was always having to watch his weight. He could gain a pound just looking at a chocolate éclair through a shop window, and the pastry in Athens had been delicious. He often envied Julia

11

bitterly, and demanded to know why she was so lucky.

On the other hand, Julia did not care much for pastry. Which always seemed to be the way. The only sweet thing she had any craving for was chewing gum. Every extra space in her suitcase had been crammed with packages of American chewing gum when they left home, and by now she was doling it out to herself only on special occasions, because her supply was getting low.

"*Souvlakia!*" said Hay, and his mouth watered. *Souvlakia* consisted of chunks of lamb roasted on thin wooden skewers about the size of an ice cream stick split in two lengthways. Each stick held five or six pieces of delicious, freshly roasted lamb, and cost three drachmas, or about ten cents. Dreams of *souvlakia* so filled Hay's head that he had almost forgotten about Nicki's mischief when the bus pulled up at a café and Mr. Kazantzakis stood up to face his passengers. He made a brief announcement which Professor Hobbs later translated as, "We stop here for fifteen minutes," pulled his cap from the shelf, and clapped it jauntily on his head.

At least, he tried to. But to his surprise, it perched on top of his bushy head of hair and slid forward down his large nose.

Annoyed by this affront to his dignity. Mr. Kazantzakis hastily tried again. He gave the cap a savage tug, and this time it stayed on, but it still looked several sizes too small.

Hay glanced at Nicki. Though he was making a

great show of rubbing his eyes and yawning, Hay knew he wasn't missing a thing. The man next to Nicki, the bus driver's friend, had also awakened. He looked at Mr. Kazantzakis and laughed. The driver glared at him and stamped off the bus. By then Nicki was busy taking down a small suitcase from the rack above his head.

The Hobbses climbed off with the rest of the passengers and made for the *souvlakia* counter in the café. The entire front of the café was open, and inside were a dozen small tables. Mr. Kazantzakis sat down at one of them, yanked off his cap, and gave it an angry inspection.

At one side behind a counter was a grill on which dozens of skewers of *souvlakia* were cooking. In a square glass case, piled up in an orderly fashion, was a huge mound of meat on sticks, ready to be grilled. Soon the Hobbs family, along with most of the other passengers, were enjoying this Levadian specialty.

Meanwhile Hay was watching Mr. Kazantzakis and Nicki. Nicki was standing off to one side, eating, and observing the bus driver out of the corner of his eye. Mr. Kazantzakis had gotten as far as feeling around inside his cap and had made a discovery. Turning down the sweatband, he pulled out the long strip of folded newspaper that had been tucked inside it.

"Blankety-blank!" cried Mr. Kazantzakis, only in Greek, and scowlingly unfolded the cause of his troubles. His friend, who had sat down with him, was watching with a wide grin. Mr. Kazantzakis

stared at the strip from his cap ,and then at the newspaper his friend had carried off the bus.

With a magnificent swipe of his hand Mr. Kazantzakis tore the newspaper from his friend's grasp,
spread it flat on the table, riffled through it, and
slapped down the piece where a page was missing.

Then a lot of shouting and hand-waving started.

"What's that all about?" Mrs. Hobbs wondered.

"Maybe there's going to be a fight!" said Julia hopefully.

"Mr. Kazantzakis is claiming the other man did something and the other man is claiming he didn't," Professor Hobbs reported, and looked at his son. "What's so funny, Hay?"

But Hay was giggling too hard to answer.

"What did he do?" asked Mrs. Hobbs.

"Something to his cap," said Professor Hobbs. "I can't quite make out what, the way he's shouting."

"That's why it looked so funny!" Julia decided.

"Now they're saying something about a boy who was sitting beside the other man."

The two men began to look around with terrible scowls on their faces. Hay looked, too. Nicki was nowhere to be seen. He had quietly disappeared.

The men stopped shouting at each other, and growled for a while about what they would do to Nicki if they ever caught him. Their dark eyes flashed ferociously under their heavy eyebrows. The black looks on their faces were enough to chill a person's blood. They looked as cruel as two villains in an opera plotting a horrible murder, probably with knives.

Then the bus driver's friend suddenly began to grin.

Then Mr. Kazantzakis began to grin.

Then they started to laugh, and nearly fell out of their chairs laughing.

"The Greeks still enjoy a clever trick, just the way they did twenty-five hundred years ago," Professor Hobbs informed his family. "That's the way they are. Wonderful people!"

Still chuckling, Hadrian Hobbs thought about Nicki. He was sorry Nicki was not going on to Delphi. He might be fun to have around—if a fellow kept his wits about him!

two

When the passengers were back in their seats again and the bus had left Levadia behind, Julia said, "That was a funny trick that boy pulled."

"You mean Nicki? Yes, it was."

"Nicki? How do you know that was his name?"

"Oh, I just know." Sometimes Hay liked to show off and mystify his sister.

"But how?" Julia persisted.

"While you had your nose in a book back in the bus station in Athens, I was listening to him talk to his friend, that's how."

"We have to study our lessons when we can," said Julia primly. They had come to Greece early in the spring, because their father had been given a special vacation for research by the Midwestern university where he was a professor of ancient history.

"Huh! You weren't studying your homework, you were reading that book about Sparta."

"Well, that's sort of lessons. That's history of ancient Greece, and Miss Quincy said to learn all I could about Greece, as well as keeping up with my school work."

"The Spartans were a pain," declared Hay. He had a fat boy's love of comfort, and therefore disliked their harsh scheme of life, which had featured plain food and endless hard exercise.

"The Spartans were very important. They were the greatest warriors of all the Greeks. They could really fight!" declared Julia, who loved fighting of all kinds. It often made her angry that she was stuck with being a girl, and with being told it was unladylike to go around punching people in the nose. "The Spartans admired clever tricks, too, like Daddy said. One time a Spartan boy stole a fox and hid it under his cloak, and when he was carrying it home a man stopped to talk to him, and while they were talking the fox got his head loose. But rather than let the man know he had stolen a fox, the boy let the fox eat his whole insides and he died!"

"I always thought that was a pretty stupid trick, myself."

"That shows how much *you* know. He was about the bravest boy that ever lived!"

"He was a nut!"

" If they had thought they were in mountains be-

18

fore they reached Levadia, they soon *knew* they were in them after they left there. The road climbed steeply, with one hairpin turn after another. The mountains were taller, grander, and more rugged. Wispy fog still swept across the road in great ragged patches, but they could see enough to know that the scenery was becoming spectacular.

"Whee!" Julia leaned across Hay, who was having his turn by the window now. "Look at *that!*"

They peered down over the edge of the road into what appeared to be a bottomless chasm.

"I'm not going to open my eyes again till we get to Delphi," their mother announced.

Out of the mist ahead appeared a flock of sheep, trotting along the road and filling it from side to side. When Mr. Kazantzakis tooted his horn importantly, the shepherds poked the sheep together with their crooks, gathering them on the inside half of the road at a point where it swung around the side of a steep rocky slope. Wheeling the bus nonchalantly to the outside edge, Mr. Kazantzakis drove past the animals. When Hay looked out the window now, it seemed as if the bus were hanging in space.

"This is the best yet. Don't look now, Mom."

"Don't even tell me about it!"

"Stop piling all over me, will you?" ordered Hay, pushing Julia, who was leaning across him again to look out.

"Well, you're getting all the best places. I didn't get to see any places where it looked like we could fall a hundred miles! It's not fair."

"I wish you'd change the subject," declared their
suffering mother. "Honestly, I must be crazy to be
here. Before we ever came over to Greece I remember reading a book by a woman who said she was

scared to death on this road every inch of the way, too!"

"Get out your worry beads, Mom," suggested Hay, but Julia reminded him it was the men, not the women, who used most of the worry beads, a great favorite in the Eastern Mediterranean world. They were small strings of smooth beads a person could slip through his fingers, round and round their string, to soothe his nerves. Several of the men on the bus held them in their hands while they chatted with each other.

"Well, you'll have to admit it's magnificent scenery, what you can see of it," said Professor Hobbs, "and wait till you see Mount Parnassus."

"What's that, Daddy?"

"It's the mountain Delphi is on, Julia. The sanctuary of Delphi, where all the ruins of the treasuries and temples are, stands on the side of a vast mountain, and looks as if it might slide straight down the side. A good deal of it has, too, in various earthquakes in the past."

Delphi began to sound like an interestingly dangerous place.

As they went on, the mist began to lift and disappear. Now they could see much farther in all directions, even though the sky remained cloudy. Before long they came to the mountain village of Arachova, and their father announced that they were now on Mount Parnassus.

"Like any big mountain, it's too big to see when you're on it, but this is it."

From there on the drive was one that Mrs. Hobbs felt anyone would be lucky to live through once in a lifetime, yet later on they learned that children from all over the area, including Delphi itself, attended high school in Arachova and traveled in a bus along that same road every day of the school year.

Before long Professor Hobbs, who had been sitting by the window ever since Levadia, was craning his neck to look ahead as he tried to remember the countryside from previous visits.

"Get ready. I'm sure we're not far from Delphi now, and I don't want you to miss the first view of it," he said. His memory was right, because a curve or two later they swept around a fold of Mount Parnassus, and there ahead they saw the sanctuary of Apollo.

three

Below the road on the left were three graceful marble columns with a fragment of the entablature still on top of them. They had once been part of a circle of columns. Around them were the ruins of many ancient buildings. Above the road, facing them, was the sanctuary of Apollo, dominated by his temple. Only a few columns of the great temple were erect, but it was astonishing how impressive they looked. Simple and powerful, with a rough, sand-colored surface, they looked as ancient as they were.

"Once there were scores of buildings and thousands of statues there," said Professor Hobbs, his eyes shining with the glory of what he was able to imagine, even though most of it was lost in the darkness of distant ages, and could never be seen again.

23

The ruins of the sanctuary stood on a shelf of land that was closed in on two sides by sheer, towering cliffs of bare rock. Where the cliffs came together at right angles they were divided by the tallest, narrowest rocky gorge the children had ever seen. This was the famous gorge of the Castalia spring.

"We should really stop at the spring and take a bath. That's what people did in ancient times before they entered the sanctuary. It was a ritual, to make them pure enough to enter."

"What a shivery idea on a day like this!" said Mrs. Hobbs. "I think I'd hold your clothes while the rest of you bathed."

"I think I'd keep you company, Mom," said Hay.

"That big white marble building ahead is the museum. That's where I hope to get a lot of information from the experts working there. I wish the French hadn't used such terribly white marble— makes the place stand out like an enormous bedsheet —but it *is* a fine museum. But now look down there, if you want to see one of the greatest views in the world."

On their right they were passing the sanctuary, most of which was high above the road, with the sheer cliffs towering above it, and somewhere in the clouds far over them the lofty snow-covered summit of Mount Parnassus. To their left the slope tumbled almost straight down into a narrow valley, on the other side of which rose another mountain, not as huge as Mount Parnassus, but high and rugged, called Cirphis.

Through the valley ran a gray ribbon of water, the river Pleistos. As they passed the museum and began to round the curve to the north that would take them to the village, less than a mile further on, they could look down and see how the valley widened out below Delphi, spreading like a fan as the Pleistos ran on through it to empty into the Gulf of Corinth, whose waters they could see in the distance a dozen miles away.

The remarkable thing about the valley was that it was filled from side to side, and all the way to the gulf, with the beautiful gray-green foliage of olive trees.

"The Sea of Olives," said Professor Hobbs, with a showmanlike wave of his hand.

The olive groves did indeed look like a sea. There were so many trees that all one could see was the tops of them blended together into endless gray-green billows. They filled every corner of the valley, and lapped up the slopes like a tide. Nobody could count all the trees, but there were at least a million. Nobody knew how old the oldest were, but some had been living for nearly a thousand years. Long before Columbus had discovered America, some were already growing below Delphi.

The village of Kastri, or Delphi, as it was more often called now, possessed one of the finest views of any town in the world. Strung along the slant of the mountainside, it looked down across the Sea of Olives and the gray ribbon that was the river Pleistos to the blue waters of the gulf, rimmed to the north by a majestic snow-capped range of peaks.

There were two streets in Delphi, and they forked near the beginning of the village. The main roadway, which was lined with hotels and shops and cafes on both sides, curved through the town on one level, while the other climbed steeply and ran parallel to it, but high above it. The bus stopped in the center of town beside a café that also served as the bus station. Near this café a flight of broad stone steps ran up the hill to connect with the street that passed through town up above.

Quite a few people were waiting for the bus to arrive. Mr. Kazantzakis bustled off to see about the unloading of the baggage from the roof, most of which was covered by tarpaulins that were still gleaming wetly from the mist. Along with the other passengers, the Hobbses filed off to stand and watch their bags be handed down.

Among those waiting Hay noticed a Greek boy about his own age. He had a mop of curly dark hair over bright dark eyes set deep above his shining olive cheeks, and he was thin and wiry, like Julia. He had a worried look as he craned his neck this way and that, trying to see the people who had not yet gotten off the bus. Hay, looking at him, caught his eye. The boy turned and began asking questions in the forthright way of all Greeks. They think nothing of asking a stranger all sorts of personal questions, and they cheerfully answer any he may ask of them.

"Hello, please," said the boy. "Are you English?"

"No, we're Americans."

"Americans! Good. My name is Kostas. What is your name?"

"Hay."

"Is this young woman your sister?" asked Kostas, and Julia giggled at being called a young woman.

"Yes. Her name's Julia."

"Is that your father and mother?"

"Yes."

"Are you going to stay in Delphi?"

"Yes, for a week."

"Good. I make you welcome to Delphi."

"Thank you. Where did you learn your English?"

"In school. And from my Uncle Giorgio. I talk it not well, but—"

"You talk it *very* well," declared Julia, looking at him shyly. She was always shy when she met strange boys, unless she could think of a good reason for kicking them in the shins, and she was getting a little old for that.

Kostas beamed at her.

"Thank you very much." He turned back to the bus. "I am looking for my cousin, but I don't see him."

Hay had a flash of intuition.

"Your cousin Nicki?"

Kostas stared at him, amazed.

"How did you know?"

"I didn't know, I just had a hunch."

"A hunch?"

"I just happened to think of it. A boy named Nicki was on the bus, but he got off at Levadia. He

27

played a funny trick on the bus driver and another man, and then disappeared."

Kostas' face lit up from ear to ear. He had beautiful white teeth, and almost every one of them was in sight.

"That's my cousin Nicki, very sure," he said, nodding vigorously. "He is a famous joke-player. Everybody wants to beat him up all the time, only he makes them laugh. He stays in Levadia, you say? He will go to visit his Uncle Loukas and his Aunt Melpemone there, and he will come on the to-morrow bus instead. I will go tell Uncle Giorgio. You must meet our Uncle Giorgio, he has the most famous shop in town, he has famous dresses for your mother. I will tell him about Nicki, and then I have to go back to school. Goodby. I hope I will see you again."

"*Herete,*" said Hay, and Julia said, "*Adio,*" both of which mean goodby in Greek. As he started to run off down the street, Kostas looked around, surprised.

"*Adio!*" he said, waved, and raced away through the crowd. Hay and Julia looked at each other, and both were grinning.

"Then maybe we haven't seen the last of Nicki after all!"

"Maybe we'll have some fun!" said Julia.

four

The hotel Professor Hobbs had chosen was a small three-story building a hundred yards or so farther on along the main street. From their rooms on the top floor they had a fine view of the Sea of Olives, the gulf, and the mountains.

It was one o'clock, and they were all hungry, but Professor Hobbs was so eager for them to see the sanctuary that he could hardly bring himself to stop and eat first.

"We'll get a quick bite of something across the street." He herded them out of the hotel toward three restaurants that were side by side and looked almost exactly alike; large square rooms with plate-glass windows across the front, plain-looking tables inside and, beyond the main room, spacious open-air pavilions overlooking the valley. Greek restaurants seldom went in for fancy decorations. Given the view that was available from the pavilions, elaborateness was not necessary.

Professor Hobbs considered the three restaurants.

"Well, let's see, let's try the middle one. I'm sure they're all about the same—one no worse than the next, and no better."

Greek food was often good, but not in the average Greek restaurant. However, the Hobbses were all hungry, and the *moussakas* tasted fine. *Moussakas* was made with ground beef and, at that time of the year, sliced potatoes. Later on, when eggplant was in season, it would be used instead of potatoes, Professor Hobbs said. "And then *moussakas* is really delicious."

"Eggplant! I'd rather have potatoes," said Julia. She was a conservative eater. Hay was more inclined to try new things than she was. She usually ordered *moussakas* wherever she went.

After lunch they walked through town toward the sanctuary. All along the main street there were shops filled with clothing and pottery, jewelry and souvenirs. Greek dresses, sheepskin coats, shawls, and kerchiefs hung outside, over boxes of fur slippers.

"I wonder where Kostas' uncle's shop is?" said Hay.

"Is Kostas the boy you were talking to?"

"Yes, Mom. He said his uncle Giorgio has the most famous shop in town, and he has famous dresses for you."

"You stay out of there, wherever it is," growled their father, but he was grinning sadly when he said it, because he knew he was wasting his breath. He knew their mother would want to look around in all the shops.

They were nearing the end of the main street when they came to a shop with a big sign over it that read:

GIORGIO MICHAELIDES

The sign was not in Greek letters, because Giorgio Michaelides wanted the tourists to have no trouble reading it.

"I'll bet that's Kostas' uncle's shop," cried Julia.

"Something tells me it is," said their father. "That woman in there seems to be trying on one of his famous dresses right now."

Inside the shop a woman who was obviously a tourist was admiring herself in a dress with some Greek designs on it. As they walked by, a dark, handsome young man was telling her in a husky voice that he had made the dress just for her.

"And I'll bet that's Giorgio," said Professor Hobbs.

Hay looked at Kostas' uncle. Then he turned to Julia.

"You know something? He reminds me of Nicki."

"He does me, too. He looks a lot like him."

"Who's this Nicki you keep talking about?" asked their father. Hay reflected that grown-ups never

31

seemed to know what was going on under their noses. He explained about Nicki, and Kostas, and Uncle Giorgio. Both his parents were quite interested. Several times they laughed.

"That Nicki sounds like a live wire, and I suspect he takes after his Uncle Giorgio. You two had better watch your step—he might be too much for you."

"I'll take a chance," said their mother loyally.

"Hay can outfox him anytime," declared Julia with equal loyalty. Even though she argued with her brother between themselves, she was always his firm ally when they had an outsider to contend with.

Leaving the village behind, they walked around the fold of Mount Parnassus that separated it from the sanctuary, and were presently passing the museum.

"We won't go in there now, we'll save that for another day," said their father. "First I want you to see the sanctuary."

"Why is it called a sanctuary, Dad? Aren't sanctuaries churches?"

"Yes, a person can seek sanctuary in a church. But in this case the whole area, the whole precinct of Apollo, as it was called, was a sanctuary. Anyone who came here was safe from harm. Even his worst enemy would not kill him while he was in the precinct of Apollo here at Delphi. In a moment now we'll come to the beginning of the Sacred Way. We'll walk along it through the sanctuary just as the pilgrims did when they came here."

"Pilgrims? You keep saying Pilgrims, Daddy. I

thought they were the people who sailed to America!"

"These were some other pilgrims, Julia. Anyone who journeys to foreign lands can be called a pilgrim."

"Then we're pilgrims!"

"The dictionary would agree with you, yes."

"Pilgrims! That's great!"

More than two hours later, they were footsore from a thorough tour. There was so much to be seen, especially when you had a father who knew a great deal about it all, that the whole place was just a jumble of ruins to Hay and Julia when they tried to think about it later. It was too much to take in on one walk.

Above the sanctuary, cradled in a steep hillside, was the amphitheater, a semicircular open-air theater, and far above it, along a path that zigzagged back and forth like a goat trail, they had come finally to the stadium. On the slope above a long, narrow, level field, and around the far end, were tiers of marble seats, still in place after nearly two thousand years.

Towering above the stadium like threatening giants rose the sheer-sided Phaidriades, the Shining Ones, the rock faces that gleamed like mirrors when the sun shone on them. Near the tops of the Shining Ones, black against the dull sky, great birds soared effortlessly in wide circles.

"The eagles of Delphi," said Professor Hobbs. "Some say they are vultures, but don't let that bother

you. At this distance they're majestic and—"

"—and ominous-looking," declared Mrs. Hobbs. Standing alone in the center of the stadium field, they drew closer together. There was no escaping the dark, savage feeling that underlay the outwardly serene atmosphere of Delphi.

"This can be dangerous country," Professor Hobbs remarked, as though sensing their thoughts. "Nobody is supposed to do any climbing anywhere on Mount Parnassus without a guide. Believe me, I wouldn't want to."

Hadrian's gaze traveled once more up the cruel sides of the Phaidriades. The tops of those rocky citadels looked impossibly remote.

From the stadium they went back to the village by another route, staying high on the slope and going over the top of the ridge that separated them from the town. When they reached the high street, children were straggling down it in twos or threes coming home from school. Among the children Hay and Julia saw their new friend.

"There's Kostas! Mom, may we wait and walk with Kostas?"

"All right, Hay. Your father and I will go on ahead. You know your way back to the hotel."

By the time Kostas reached them, he was alone. He looked pleased to see them again, and to see them waiting for him.

They told him what they had been doing, and then Kostas said, "You come to the tomorrow bus

35

when my cousin Nicki comes from Levadia, all right?"

"That's a good idea. We'll be there."

"Then we will go to see my Uncle Giorgio, because he is waiting till Nicki comes to tell something exciting."

"What do you mean?"

"He has a letter from Uncle Petros in America."

"You have an uncle in America?"

"For a long time," said Kostas proudly, as they started down the steps toward the main street. "Since the great war, almost twenty years ago. Uncle Petros was in the Resistance. He was a—what do you call them. . . ?"

"A guerrilla?"

"Yes, a guerrilla fighter. He killed many Nazi Germans, and when they tried to find him he hid in a cave high on the mountain, where those stupid soldiers never could find him."

Kostas stopped and looked around. He lowered his voice in a very exciting and mysterious way.

"There is something in the cave. Uncle Giorgio won't tell me what, but when Nicki comes Uncle Giorgio will tell. Maybe you will go, too?"

"You mean, up to the cave?"

"Yes."

Hay thought about the Shining Ones, so high and sheer that eagles made their nests on them. He and Julia exchanged a wide-eyed, delighted glance, with a delicious tingle of fright traveling up their spines. They stared again at Kostas.

"You mean it? You're sure it would be all right?"

Kostas was very grand about it. He stood back and waved his arm in a wide sweep.

"I invite you!"

five

The next day started with a visit to the museum. Professor Hobbs could not wait any longer to show them its treasures. These proved to be more interesting than the children had expected, especially the prize statue of them all, a bronze figure of a charioteer.

The bronze was the dark green color it turns as it ages. Tall and erect, the Charioteer had the look of a victor. His face, though calm and composed, seemed marvelously alive. One of his arms was missing, but the other was thrust before him, holding the reins in a convincing manner. He *looked* like a youth who could easily make four powerful horses do his bidding and act as a team.

"This is one of the most famous statues in the

world. Next time we're up in the sanctuary I'll show you exactly where it was found. It was buried by a landslip after an earthquake a couple of thousand years ago, and not found again until 1898. Back in the First Century A.D., a drain was dug from the amphitheater down past the spot where the Charioteer was found. At that time, Greece was part of the Roman Empire, and the Romans were in charge here in Delphi. If they had dug the drain just a few inches closer, the statue would have been discovered then and there, and they would have carried it away, probably back to some villa near Rome. It wouldn't have been here for us to enjoy."

The Charioteer had a room all to himself. The only other things in it were some cases containing fragments of the chariot pole, two hind legs of horses, a horse's tail and hoof, a few sections of the reins, and the arm of a child. Originally the group of which the Charioteer was a part had included a full-sized chariot and four horses, as well as some other human figures.

"The Charioteer stood in the chariot high on a pedestal, where nobody could possibly see his feet, and yet look at them. Perfect in every detail. That's the way a great artist works. He never skimps."

There were many other statues, and various smaller objects, and also some friezes from the pediments of temples that had once stood in the sanctuary. Julia particularly liked the scenes shown on these, because everybody was fighting. If the Greeks and Trojans weren't fighting over the body of

Patroclos, then Athena was fighting the giants.

"Athena! Now, there's a goddess you would have enjoyed being, Julia," said her father. "With you around, the Greeks would have licked the Trojans in half the time!"

Hay kept his eye on the hour, and well before twelve-thirty he and Julia were walking back into town to meet Kostas and wait for the bus. As they passed Uncle Giorgio's shop, they looked in to see if their new friend was there, but did not see him. What they did see was Uncle Giorgio deep in conversation with a pretty, dark-haired girl, whose hand he was holding across a counter. They paused in the doorway to have a good look at him, and after a moment he noticed them there. It was immediately obvious that he did not like to be gawked at by passing children at such a time.

"Boo!" he shouted in his husky voice. "Go away!"

He looked so fierce they nearly fell over each other as they turned to run.

"Now we've made Uncle Giorgio mad before we've even met him!" panted Hay as they scuttled up the street. "That was a mistake!"

"Well, how were we to know he'd mind?"

"He probably won't even let us in his shop now. Darn you, why did you have to stop, anyway?"

"*Me* stop? You stopped first!"

"I did not. You did."

"*You* did."

They were still wasting their breath arguing about this when they reached the bus station. Kostas was already there. He said good morning to them in Greek.

"*Kali mera!*"

"*Kali mera,* Kostas. Well, we've fixed things now," grumbled Hay, and told him what had happened. Kostas' wide grin got a good workout.

"That's my Uncle Giorgio, all right. But don't worry. He never stays mad long. I tell you what we will do, we will tell him your mother wants to see his famous dresses, and then he will have to be nice."

Julia nodded thoughtfully.

"We could do that. Then only our *father* will be mad."

"I'm hungry. I wonder if they have any *baklava* in this café?" said Hay. However, before he could go looking for the flaky honey cakes that are a favorite sweet in Greece, the bus from Athens surprised everybody by showing up on time. As it came to a stop in front of them, Kostas began to jump up and down.

"There's Nicki!"

Through the windows Hay could see the tall boy with the foxy face stand up and lift his suitcase from the rack. It was the same Nicki, no doubt about that. When he stepped off the bus, his strong white teeth flashed at the sight of Kostas. As for Kostas, his excitement made it plain that here was his special hero. Nicki accepted his cousin's hug like a film star graciously permitting his public to adore him.

Kostas seized his suitcase, eager for the honor of carrying it, and said, "This is Hay and Julia. They're Americans. They were on the bus with you yesterday."

"Yes, I remember."

"That was a funny trick you played on the driver," said Hay, laughing.

Nicki stared at him. He looked insulted.

"Trick?"

"Sure! I saw you take the man's newspaper, and put a piece in Mr. Kazantzakis' cap."

The minute he said this, Hay wished he hadn't. His own tendency to show off had betrayed him. Nicki was obviously annoyed, and Hay realized at once what he was angry about. Nicki did not like the idea that anyone had seen him do it! That made him feel less clever.

"You saw me, did you?"

"Yes. After you left, Mr. Kazantzakis and his friend figured out it had to be you, but you really fooled them good," Hay added lamely. The damage was already done, however. Nicki continued to look sour.

"That was a very funny trick, Nicki," said Kostas, too happy to notice anything wrong. "But come on, we're all going to Uncle Giorgio's!"

"All of us?" said Nicki.

"Yes!" Kostas rattled off his news in one breathless rush. "Uncle Giorgio has a letter from Uncle Petros, there is something in the cave on the mountain, we are going up there and I asked them to come with us."

Nicki almost stopped.

"You what?" He glared at Hay, then turned sharply to Kostas. "Does Uncle Giorgio know?"

43

"Not yet, but—"

"He won't like that!"

Kostas shot an embarrassed glance at Hay, and began to talk to his cousin in Greek. Hay and Julia trailed along uncomfortably. Fine thing! thought Hay. First they made Uncle Giorgio mad at them, and now he had made Nicki mad, too! The trip to the cave was something they could probably just as well forget about, because they would never be allowed to go along now.

Kostas was still trying to reason with Nicki when they reached the shop, but then the argument broke off, because Uncle Giorgio rushed to the door to greet the new arrival. Their uncle had been busy charming two American ladies who were looking at his famous dresses, but he stopped long enough to hug Nicki.

"Nicki! I'm so glad to see you! Come in, come in! I'm very busy—two nice lady customers, and a friend in the other room. I'm busy, very busy, but come in and wait, come in, come in!"

Uncle Giorgio was so absorbed in welcoming his nephew that he did not even notice Hay and Julia slip inside—and certainly they were trying to be as inconspicuous as possible. With one accord they sidled toward the archway that led into the other room, to keep out of the way until Kostas had a chance to speak to his uncle about them.

As they entered the room, the beautiful girl who was leaning on a showcase looking at some costume jewelry glanced up at them and smiled. They had expected the pretty dark-haired girl, but this one was a blonde.

"Why, it's not the same girl!" blurted Julia.

The blonde girl's smile faded.

"What?"

"Er—"

The girl's blue eyes narrowed. She beckoned to Julia with one long, tapering index finger.

"Come here, little one."

"Er—yes, ma'm?" Julia walked forward on stiff legs, the way she would have entered a principal's office.

"What do you mean, not the same girl?"

Julia gulped. "Well, I only meant not the same as that other one."

"*What* other one?"

"I m-mean, that other girl a while ago had dark hair, and—"

Uncle Giorgio had been rushing about the shop in every direction, trying to do everything at once, but now he suddenly appeared. He stopped long enough to beam in at the girl.

"I'll only be a moment, Freda, darling. Please wait!"

Freda's blue eyes flashed Scandinavian lightning.

"Don't darling *me*, you playing boy!" she said, not getting the expression quite right—she must have meant "playboy"—and strode out of the shop with her nose in the air.

Uncle Giorgio stared after her, thunderstruck. Then he looked down at Hay and Julia and recognized them. Not only recognized them, but realized that in some way they must be responsible . . .

Uncle Giorgio turned a dangerous red color. Out came his worry beads. And even as he twiddled them through the fingers of one hand, he pointed forcibly with the other at the door.

"Out! *Out!* And stay out!"

six

Hay and Julia shot out of the shop like two bandits out of a bank. Hay had never been so fleet of foot in his life. And even then he had all he could do to keep up with his speeding sister.

He did not even shout "big mouth" at her, the way he felt like doing. There was no time for that now. The important thing was to try to think their way out of the mess they were in. He was doing that as fast as he could.

"There she is!" He pointed at the girl Freda, who was rapidly disappearing up the street with long goddess-like strides. "Come on! Maybe that other girl was his cousin. Anyway, we're going to *say* she was!"

"Okay, Hay," said Julia, as they ran after Freda.

At such times, if Hay had a plan, she had learned not to argue or hesitate, but to cooperate.

"Miss Freda! Hey, Miss Freda!" called Hay. He waved his arms beseechingly as the girl shot a stormy glance back their way. Surprised to see such a plump boy running so hard, she stopped and waited.

"We're sorry, Miss Freda, we were only talking about his little cousin!" panted Hay.

Freda's eyes flickered.

"Little . . . cousin?" she said coolly, but she did sound interested.

"That's right!"

"Little cousin, you say? How little?"

"Well . . . not very big. Not very old, either."

"Ha! With him, she wouldn't have to be very old!"

"Yes, but his *cousin!* She was in his shop a while ago, and we saw her, and that's all," said Hay. He hoped he was telling a white lie, the kind that doesn't hurt or count, at least not very much. "Please! If you don't come back, we're going to be in awful trouble. Was he ever mad at us!"

Freda gazed down at his earnest, chubby face, and a dimple appeared in her cheek. Her beautiful blue eyes began to twinkle. Then she threw back her head and loosed a free, wholehearted bellow. It was startling to hear a hands-on-hips, all-out laugh from such a girl, except that it had a sort of Norse-goddess-like ring, at that.

"So that's it! Well, all right. I wouldn't want to get you into trouble," she said and glanced down the

48

street. Hay had a suspicion that she was glad of an excuse to return. "Come on, we'll go back and make peace with that *odjur*."

"*Odjur?* What's that?"

"That's Swedish. It means—what do you say?—monster!"

"Are you Swedish?"

"Yes. I'm a student of archaeology at a university. There are twenty of us here from Sweden, and two professors. We came today."

"And already you know Uncle Giorgio?"

The dimple reappeared in her cheek, and she laughed again.

"We were here last week, too. We made a field trip and came back."

Freda asked them about themselves, and by the time they had answered her questions they were back at the shop. Hay might have held the door for her at another time, but this time he rushed ahead to get in the first words. Uncle Giorgio was in the midst of a conversation with his two American lady customers, and his worry beads were still busy in his hand. He had something to worry about, too. The ladies seemed about to walk out in a huff.

"I'm sorry I lost my temper about those two nice American children," he was saying, "but—"

"Mr. Giorgio! We told her about seeing your little cousin with you, and everything's all right!" cried Hay, startling all three of them. Uncle Giorgio blinked down at him, but his quick mind was working rapidly, responding to Hay's message.

"Little cousin?" he repeated. "Oh, yes! My little cousin! Well! Well, thank you very much—er—"

"Hay."

"Hay."

"And Julia."

"And Julia," repeated Uncle Giorgio. He glanced with melting eyes at Freda. "I'm so sorry you misunderstood—"

"I don't think I did, you *odjur!*" said Freda, but she said it with a grin.

"That means monster," said Julia helpfully.

"Will you be *quiet?*" barked Hay, and everybody laughed.

"Well, perhaps we'll come back," said one of the American ladies, looking less severe. But she laid aside the blue dress she had been holding. "However, I don't think I'll try anything on just now."

Once his brain was working at top speed, Hay was sometimes good for more than one inspiration. Here were these two ladies, about to walk out of the shop without buying anything, if someone did not stop them. Hay had an idea.

"My mother wants to try on your famous dresses, Mr. Giorgio," he said. "She knows all about them. I think she read about them in our magazines at home, didn't she, Julia?"

"Gosh, yes!"

"Did she?" cried Uncle Giorgio, delighted.

"Well, that's what she said. I guess she'll want to buy one, all right."

The American lady was listening. She was also

looking thoughtful. She began to finger the blue dress again.

"Oh, maybe while I'm here I *should* try this one on, Cora," she said to her companion.

"I don't see why not," said Cora. "Maybe I'll try on the red one myself."

By the time each of the American ladies had bought a dress and left the store, Uncle Giorgio was feeling different about Hay and Julia. Quite different. He had sent a long-faced Nicki out to buy *baklava* and *lemonada* for everybody, and had declared the Hobbs children his honorary niece and nephew.

"So you just made that up about the magazines in America, Hay?"

"I'm afraid so, Uncle Giorgio."

"Well, I'm sorry to hear that, but just the same it only makes you twice as clever, to think of saying such a thing. *Anybody* can say something that's true, but it takes a clever person to say something that has a little imagination in it. Besides, don't worry— someday the magazines of America *will* tell your nice ladies about my famous dresses!" Uncle Giorgio predicted, and his dark eyes flashed like beacons in his handsome face under the glossy black hair.

"Do you know how I started? With nothing! Almost nothing, anyway. My family—Kostas' family— Nicki's family—all the Michaelides own olive trees. Always when I was a boy I worked among the olive trees. It was hard work. Hot! But always I wanted to

51

design those beautiful clothes, and finally my father gave me three hundred drachmas and said, 'Here! Go find out how to design those beautiful clothes!' Three hundred drachmas! Not much money. To-day I get a thousand drachmas for one dress—you just saw! Well, I took my three hundred drachmas and went to Athens and studied and worked, and now I own my own shop, and lady tourists from all over the world buy my famous dresses!"

This account of his success story was so stirring that it seemed only right to clap and cheer when he had finished. Uncle Giorgio took a bow, sat down, and sipped his *lemonada* like a statesman who had just concluded an important speech. Freda, who had joined in the applause, glanced at her watch and said she really did have to go this time, to eat lunch with her group from the university.

"But you will come back tonight, and as soon as I close the shop we will go somewhere?" implored Uncle Giorgio.

"All right." Freda stopped in the doorway and looked back with a teasing glint in her blue eyes. "And why don't you bring your little cousin along?"

"Please! She's busy!"

Freda laughed and strode away up the street. Uncle Giorgio stood stroking his jaw for a moment, lost in thought. Then he cocked his eye at Hay.

"That was good thinking about the little cousin, too, even though she didn't believe it," he remarked.

Nicki looked on glumly, sourer than ever. Hay might have made a hit with Uncle Giorgio, but not with him. He did not like having another boy get so much credit for being clever when he was around.

All this time Kostas had been hoping to bring up the real reason they were all there. He did not wait any longer.

"Now! Uncle Giorgio, what about the letter? . . . I told them about it and asked them to go with us," he added, when his uncle glanced at Hay and Julia. "Is that all right?"

Uncle Giorgio took no time in deciding.

"Of course that's all right!" he said, and nobody but Hay noticed how Nicki folded his arms and blew out a sigh of disgust.

"Well, then, what's it all about?" asked Kostas.

Uncle Giorgio sipped his *lemonada* and set it down. He peered outside.

"No customers are coming. All the tourists are going to lunch. There is time, I think." He turned and walked toward the back of the shop. "I will get Uncle Petros' letter."

seven

Except for Nicki, who was trying very hard to be
nonchalant and worldly, it was a wide-eyed group
that faced Uncle Giorgio as he unfolded the letter.

"Kostas told you about my brother Petros, eh?"

"Yes."

"He was a great fighter in the Resistance. And
now for twenty years he has been in your country."

He smoothed the letter out flat on the showcase
he was standing behind.

"He writes it in English," he informed them
proudly, proud both of his brother's English, and his
own ability to read it. "It is a great thing to know
English. It helps me more than anything to sell my
famous dresses. It helps me to talk to Freda, too, because it is the only language we both know. She

knows very little modern Greek, and I don't know one word of Swedish. Except *odjur*," he added with a quick grin. "Well, now for the letter. Uncle Petros says:

" 'Dear Giorgio, For many years I have not thought much about the great war and the cave where some of us hid during the fighting, and I forgot all about something I left in it until this week. This week I went to a museum and happened to look at the Greek rooms there. All at once I hit myself and said, Petros, you are a fathead, as we say here in America, a fathead who forgets everything. You found that very old gold ring that time when you were digging a grave to put a German in, and you hid the ring in the cave and it will still be there, because even today not many know where that cave is and even then nobody could find the ring unless I told him where to look.' "

After a sentence as long as that, Uncle Giorgio had to stop for a moment to catch his breath. That gave them all a chance to stare around at each other. Even Nicki had forgotten he was trying to be nonchalant. Now he looked excited, too. Hay recalled some of the ancient gold rings from Mycenae and Crete they had seen in the Athens museum, and knew how highly prized they were.

Uncle Giorgio resumed reading.

" 'So I thought I would tell you where I left the ring in the cave, Giorgio, and some day you could go up and get it and give it to the museum to put in a glass case with a card saying it was given by the

Michaelides family of Delphi.' "

Hay could not contain himself at this news.

"That's wonderful! My father will be so excited he won't know what to do!"

"Your father? Why?"

Hay explained who his father was. Uncle Giorgio was greatly impressed, because Greeks have a high regard for learning and for professors.

"But don't tell him until we have it," he warned. "Don't tell anybody, or somebody else might try to get there first."

"We won't!"

"That is why I won't read to you the part of Uncle Petros' letter telling where to find the ring in the cave. That way nobody can let it slip out. When we are ready to go, then I will read the rest of the letter to you."

"When can we go?" asked Kostas.

"Well, I can't leave the shop for a couple of days, but the first day there are not many tourists in town I will leave Spyros Papadopoulos in charge and we will go."

"Who?" asked Hay, marveling at the name.

"Spyros Papadopoulos. He's my assistant."

Uncle Giorgio reminded them again that no one was to say anything about the ring, and the meeting broke up. Kostas had to return to school, and of course Nicki had not even been home yet to see his family. Hay and Julia walked to the steps with Kostas and then on to the hotel to meet their parents and go to lunch.

The weather was so fine that they were able to sit out on the restaurant's pavilion overlooking the nubbly green carpet of olive trees in the deep valley.

"Well, was Nicki on the bus?"

"Yes, Dad."

"How was he?"

Hay shrugged. *"Etsi-ketsi,"* he said, using a favorite Greek expression. It meant "so-so," and that was the way he felt about Nicki Michaelides.

"Only *etsi-ketsi?*"

Hay explained what had happened, and his father understood.

"Of course. He didn't *want* anyone to see him do his trick. He thought he was too slick for that. Well, don't worry. He'll get over it. Anything else new?"

Hay was ready for that question, and knew he had to be careful answering it. Yesterday they had not mentioned Kostas' invitation to go along to the cave because they were afraid their parents would say it was too dangerous. Now that Uncle Giorgio was planning to lead the expedition, their parents would probably say it was all right to go, only now Hay couldn't tell them the whole story because he could not mention the ring! Life was complicated. But then he chuckled. There was no reason not to tell some of it.

"We had *everybody* mad at us for a while," he said, and explained about the dark-haired girl and Freda, with the usual interruptions from Julia. Their parents enjoyed the story.

"That was all very funny, except for the part when you said your mother wanted to buy one of his famous dresses," declared their father when they had finished.

"We knew you'd be mad about that," said Julia.

58

"I suppose I'll *have* to look at his dresses now," said Mrs. Hobbs with a happy expression. Professor Hobbs groaned and pulled out his worry beads.

"I wish Nicki wasn't mad," said Julia.

"Maybe we can do something about that," said Mrs. Hobbs. "Let's see . . . What day is tomorrow? Isn't it Saturday?"

Professor Hobbs brought out his pocket calendar. On long trips it is often hard to remember which day is which.

"Yes, so it is."

"I wonder if Kostas has to go to school on Saturdays?"

"I don't think so. Why?"

"Well, we could take a picnic lunch up to the stadium, and ask the boys to join us."

"Great!" said Hay. But then he frowned. "Maybe Nicki won't come, though."

"Maybe he won't, but maybe he will. All you can do is ask him."

"Fine. Now, in the meantime," said Professor Hobbs, with that eager light coming into his eyes again, "what say we amble down to the precinct of Athena Pronaia? We haven't seen that yet, and there are some things I want to point out to you . . ."

Mrs. Hobbs sighed.

"There's no holding your father, children. But don't worry, he'll soon be busy at the museum, and then we'll get some rest!"

During lunch they had looked down on the billowing sea of gray-green foliage. Now Hay and Julia were under it, looking up at the twisting branches and thick-set leaves.

While their parents were resting during their tour of the ruins of Athena Pronaia, on the rim of the valley below the sanctuary, the children had wandered away. They had followed a path that sloped down from one side of the area and quickly became lost among the olive trees where it was hard going, because each tree was surrounded by a circular embankment of earth, to hold the water when it rained.

"No wonder it's difficult to raise olives," said Hay, as they scrambled over the rough ground.

"At least it's not hot now," said Julia. It was almost chilly under the thick foliage. They sat down and looked around them in silence for a moment, enjoying the shaded, mysterious tunnels of shadow that ran off in every direction.

"I like Delphi, Hay."

"So do I. Sometimes it's almost creepy, as if maybe some of those Greek gods did hang around here once."

"It wouldn't surprise *me*." Julia picked up a clod of dirt and threw it at the thick trunk of an ancient tree. It struck and burst with a satisfying plunk.

"Cut that out," said Hay lazily. "Maybe that tree was here before Columbus."

"Columbus wasn't here."

"Ha-ha, funny joke."

"Bet I can hit that tree three times out of three."

"Bet you can't."

She did.

"Hay."

"Huh?"

"I hope Nicki comes to the picnic."

"Huh!"

"Don't you want him to?"

Hay shrugged. "I guess so." He rose and stretched, yawning. "Well, we'd better go back and listen to some more stuff about ruins."

"I guess we should. Might as well let Daddy finish."

Kostas was delighted to hear about the picnic.

"I will come!"

"What about Nicki?"

"I will tell him."

"Do you think he'll come?"

Kostas' wide grin brightened the day as they walked down the steps in the center of town.

"If there is going to be something to eat, he will come."

"There will be plenty to eat."

"Then he will come!"

eight

At midday Hay and Julia were waiting outside the museum, looking at the Roman mosaic floor. All sorts of strange animals and birds and fishes were pictured by its bits of colored stone. They had already spent half an hour earlier in the day arguing about what each creature was supposed to be.

When the Greek boys did not appear, they were concerned. But then they reminded themselves that Greeks seldom worried about being on time.

"At least Kostas will come. I'm sure of that," said Hay.

But then, around the bend in the road, here came both of them. So Kostas had been right, and so had their mother when she said, "There's nothing like food to make boys forget their differences." Nicki greeted them in his grand manner, as much as to say they were all small children compared to him; but at least he was not looking sour.

Soon their parents came out of the museum. Professor Hobbs was carrying a picnic basket that looked promisingly heavy. When Hay had introduced Nicki and Kostas, they began their climb up the path that led through the sanctuary and on up to the stadium. The Hobbses asked Nicki a lot of questions about his school in Athens, and Nicki acted very grown up as he answered them. His manners were perfect—too perfect, as far as Hay was concerned. But still, he was glad Nicki had come. At least it was better than not having him along. He only hoped Nicki would not eat too much.

When they finally reached the heights on which the stadium was perched, Hay forgot about Nicki and food for an instant or two. There was something magical about coming over that last slope of the path and seeing the stadium ahead through the remains of the arch that had once been its entrance. The long, narrow field lengthened out in front of him, with the seats rising around it, just the way they did when they were full of Greek and Roman spectators waiting to see the great athletes race and jump and throw the javelin and the discus.

"Well, it's too early to eat yet," said his father. though Hay would not necessarily have agreed with him, "but I have an idea. Why don't we start something new? Why don't we celebrate the first Children's Olympics ever held in old Herodias Atticus' stadium? We'll have races, and prizes, and a grand march into the stadium—everything!"

The children exchanged a variety of glances. Julia looked delighted. Nicki looked puzzled. Kostas looked ready for anything. Hay looked uneasy.

"What kind of races?" he asked.

"Well, let me think . . . I've got it! We have a number of hard-boiled eggs in yonder lunch basket, have we not, Mrs. Hobbs?"

"Quite a number, yes."

"And we have several of those nasty little plastic spoons which I ordinarily detest, but which in this case will come in very handy?"

"We do."

"Splendid. Then the first race will be an egg-in-spoon race, which should please you, Hay, since it requires skill more than speed, and you and I are not built for speed," said Professor Hobbs, patting his own ample breadbasket. "Now, let's see. For this we don't want a long course. Across the field and back will be about right. Good! And the judges can make use of the judges' seats."

Hay was half-inclined to glare at him. His father had not suddenly thought of having races, he had planned them ahead! But on the other hand, Hay was grateful for the *kind* of contest his father had thought up, because it did call for skill, as he had said, rather than speed—balance, to be exact, and Hay had an excellent sense of balance. He could carry an egg from here to Athens without dropping it, even on one of those little plastic spoons.

His mother was already producing their equipment from the basket. She handed them each an egg and a spoon, and almost at once, even before his father demonstrated, Nicki and Kostas got the idea.

"Now, then. Mrs. Hobbs and I will go sit in the judges' seats. You four will go outside the stadium and enter, two by two, in the grand march when the music starts."

"What music, Daddy?"

"Julia, how can you ask? *I* will furnish the music. I'm very good at that. My imitation of a thirty-piece brass band is known all over the world, wherever music-lovers gather."

"Oh, Daddy!" said Julia, whinnying at him self-consciously. She secretly thought he was funny, even though she sometimes tried to pretend otherwise because she was always afraid other children would not think so. But Nicki and Kostas were both enjoying themselves, and fell into the spirit of the occasion. With great pomp and circumstance Professor Hobbs led his wife to the central seats in the first row, which had backs and were scooped out much like modern contour chairs. They were actually the same places of honor occupied by judges at games held two thousand years earlier. When the Hobbses had seated themselves, the professor waved his hand in a manner worthy of a Roman emperor.

"Let the games begin!"

And to the stately rhythm of his imitation brass band the procession entered the field, two athletes marching in front, and two behind, side by side.

"That giggling will have to stop, or somebody is going to be thrown to the lions," announced the emperor. "All right now, line up in one row, facing the other side of the stadium. Now, you're to balance your egg in your spoon, and go as far as you can, over and back. The first one to touch the wall on this side wins. If you drop your egg, you have to stop, pick it up, and put it back on your spoon before you start moving ahead again. Ready? . . . Set . . . Go!"

Hay knew better than to hurry. Holding his spoon ahead of him, he walked at a smooth, easy pace, while the others rushed to take the lead. And each of the others, before reaching the other side of the stadium, dropped his egg at least once.

By the time he started back toward the finish line, Hay was well in the lead, with the other three straggling behind. Nicki, by a narrow margin, was last.

Carefully Hay eased forward, with the fire of victory throbbing in his veins. Behind him he could hear the others, not far behind, but far enough so that they could never catch him now. He kept his eye on his egg, secure in its spoon.

"Look out! There's a snake!" cried Nicki.

Hay's egg shot convulsively into space as he leaped into the air with his frightened eyes searching the ground beneath him. All he saw was a crooked black twig about two feet long, but by then it was too late. His egg was on the ground somewhere, and while he looked around wildly for it, a tall figure went slowly by.

"The winner—Nicki Michaelides!" cried the em-

peror. Hay looked up to see Nicki leaning against the wall and gazing at the rest of them with an expression that pretended to be contrite.

"*Lipame poli.* I'm very sorry. It was only a stick; I thought it was a snake."

Professor Hobbs was holding his sides and gasping with laughter.

"I swear, I think you children jumped a foot off the ground when he said that! All three of your eggs were in the air at once. Nicki, you're a rascal, but you win!"

Hay had never been so outraged.

"That's not fair!" he cried, as the emperor came down from the seat of honor. But then his father turned his way and quickly did something that only Hay could see, and which made everything all right. He winked.

"Certainly it's fair. All's fair in love and war and egg-and-spoon races," he declared, while the irritation drained out of Hay. He stopped being angry the instant he realized that he and his father had a secret: they were giving Nicki his chance to be clever! He looked at Nicki and saw how well his father's plan was working. The boy was so satisfied with himself that he was even ready to be pleased with Hay, too, if Hay would let him. So Hay let him.

"Okay, Nicki, you win!" he said, and exchanged a quick, approving glance with his father.

"The next and final race," said Professor Hobbs, "will be a relay. Nicki and Hay will be one team, and Julia and Kostas the other, with Kostas getting a head-start for the first lap."

He picked up the stick Nicki had pretended was a snake, and broke it in two.

"Here you are. Here's half a snake for each of you, for your relay batons." He gave the pieces to the Greek boys. "Nicki, you come down to the starting line, and Julia and Hay, you go up to the other end of the field. I'll mark off ten paces for Kostas' head-start. I think that ought to be about right."

"You'd better beat Kostas enough to give *me* a head-start on Julia, Nicki, or we'll never win, because she's fast," said Hay.

"Don't worry, I will!"

"He won't!" said Kostas.

Hay and Julia jogged down to the far end of the field. It was a long way. Hay thought about running all that distance, and could not work up much enthusiasm for the idea. His father had made him Nicki's partner on purpose, of course, and that meant he had to try extra hard.

They lined up about ten yards from the seats at the end of the stadium, to give the other runners room to stop in after they passed the batons. They watched their father pace off the ten steps and place Kostas for the start.

"Where we're standing will be the finish line," called Professor Hobbs. "Ready! . . . Set . . . Go!"

Hay felt he had never seen a livelier cricket of a runner than Kostas. He seemed to flash over the ground, so that even Nicki's long legs did not gain on him as rapidly as Hay had hoped. What Hay wanted

69

was about half a field's lead on Julia.

"Come on, Nicki, *run!*"

"Come on, Kostas!"

Slowly—much too slowly to suit Hay—Nicki drew even with Kostas and passed him. But he was not nearly far enough ahead when Hay stretched his arm wildly to take the baton Nicki was holding out. Nevertheless, both Nicki and Kostas were a credit to their ancestors who had once raced over that same field. They were giving the race everything they had.

The baton was in his hand, and Hay was running, thudding along to the best of his pear-shaped ability. He ran and ran, and now he could hear Julia's light feet fast behind him. His blood pounded in his ears, he heard his family's shouts, and then he had a mystic impression of shouts doubled and redoubled. It was as if the age-old stadium seats were filled again with Greeks and Romans roaring encouragement. At another time he might have given up, sure that Julia would beat him as always, but now the spirit of that ghostly roar seemed to press him forward. Instead of slowing down, he found a mysterious reserve of strength and determination that made him run just a bit harder, just a bit faster . . . just enough to send him across the finish line inches ahead of an astonished Julia.

With cheers of praise ringing in his ears Hay collapsed on the ground in a pudgy, panting heap. He was all ready to model for one of those statues of dying athletes. But instead he found himself enjoying the heady feeling of victory. Before he had caught his breath enough to get up, the others were all standing around him, laughing and congratulating him on his magnificent effort.

"You are a real Greek!" said Nicki, and that made him feel especially good.

"Well, now," said Professor Hobbs, "Nicki was a winner in both events, so that makes him the Olympic champion of the first Children's Olympics. Climb up on the pedestal, and we'll take your picture."

"Be the Charioteer!" cried Julia.

Grinning as they all applauded, Nicki climbed up on the stone wall in front of the seats. Behind him towered the Shining Ones, and above them soared a single eagle, black against the sky. Nicki drew himself up straight and tall, like the Charioteer, and as he did his face became, for a moment, calm and composed. He must have been thinking about how the Charioteer looked, and how he must have felt. They stared up at the boy, and held their breath as Mrs. Hobbs took the picture, because the amazing thing was that suddenly Nicki did look like the Charioteer. Tall and proud, holding his hand out exactly the way the Charioteer did, he gazed with his level Greek eyes into the blue distances above the sanctuary of Delphi, and time seemed to roll back twenty-five centuries.

The camera clicked, and the spell was broken. Nicki jumped down, and they had their picnic.

nine

One trouble with traveling in the spring was that there were still school lessons to think about. When the picnic was over, Mrs. Hobbs reminded the children of this grim fact.

"Don't forget, I want you to put in the rest of this afternoon on your studies. You're getting too far behind."

"Do we have to? Today, the only day Kostas doesn't have to go to school?"

"He doesn't have to go tomorrow, either."

"Well, tomorrow, but—"

"And you heard what Nicki said. They have to help their uncle this afternoon, don't you, Nicki?"

"Yes, he wants us to run some errands."

Hay made the best bargain he could.

"May we just walk back to the shop with Nicki and Kostas?"

"Yes, you may, but keep on going, to the hotel. I'm going to stay here and read for a while, and then I'll come back and see how you're doing. And I'd better find something doing. I want to find two heads bent industriously over schoolbooks."

There was no use arguing with her when she started talking like that. Their father ambled off down the path to the museum, and the children took a higher route over the ridge behind the stadium, which led them across a rocky slope past the ruins of the ancient fortress of Philomenos, above Agia Ilias, a small church that gave the hill its name.

"What do you have to study?" Nicki asked as they walked along.

"Algebra, and I hate it," said Hay.

"I have to study geography, and I hate that," said Julia. "I don't see why I have to study geography when I'm *in* geography, anyway!" she declared, sweeping her hand around her. "If Greece isn't geography, I'd like to know what is!"

"What country are you studying?"

Julia sighed. "Norway. Personally, I don't care one bit how many sardines that country exports. I don't even like them."

"I don't exactly hate algebra, but it's certainly not my best subject," said Hay.

"He only gets about eighty in it," sniffed his sister.

"Eighty! I wish I could do that well. Kostas is good at arithmetic. I'm taking geometry now, and my

73

geometry teacher, Mr. Konstantinopoulos, is a bore."

Vying with one another to recall teachers who were bores or a big pain, or both, they passed the time pleasantly until they came within sight of the shop. At that point an outburst up ahead interrupted their conversation.

A short, squat man came hurrying out, and turned to shout back into the shop. He had small, glittering eyes, and an enormous mustache. Having done his shouting, he stumped away up the street angrily, while Uncle Giorgio appeared at the door to shout after *him*. The angry man turned and made a gesture at Uncle Giorgio, who made the same motion back at him. It did not look like a compliment. Nor did the loud remarks sound exactly flattering.

Nicki and Kostas exchanged a troubled look.

"What's Papadopoulos mad about?"

"Is that Spyros Papadopoulos?" asked Hay, remembering the impressive name of Uncle Giorgio's assistant.

"No, that's *Stephanos* Papadopoulos."

Still fuming, Uncle Giorgio glanced up and down the street like a rooster ready to fight anyone. He saw the children coming, and beckoned urgently.

"Come in here!"

They filed into the shop behind him.

"What was Stephanos Papadopoulos angry about, Uncle Giorgio?"

"That no-good!" Uncle Giorgio had taken out his worry beads, and they were working overtime.

"When I heard he was Papadopoulos, I thought he was Spyros Papadopoulos, your assistant," said Hay. "No, this is his uncle. There are many, many

Papadopouloses in Greece. One too many, if you ask me! Stephanos is a—what is the American word, Nicki?"

"A racketeer?"

Uncle Giorgio laughed briefly. "Well, not quite that. But he's—in the shade. What is the expression . . . ?"

"A shady character?" suggested Hay.

"That's it! A shady character. Always looking out for a way to make a fast money."

"A fast buck."

"Yes, a fast buck. Now he wants to buy the ring! In some way he heard about the ring." Fiercely Uncle Giorgio inspected the circle of faces that surrounded him. "Which one of you talked about the ring?"

"I didn't!"

"I didn't!"

"Not me!"

"I *certainly* didn't!" declared Julia.

"Well, somebody did, because Stephanos was in here trying to find out about it. And what would he do with it, if he could get his hands on it? I'll tell you what he would do with it, that shady character! He would sell it to a collector to smuggle it out of the country, that's what he would do with it!"

Hay and Julia did not need to have this matter explained to them. From listening to their father, they knew it was against Greek law for any ancient treasures found there to be taken out of the country.

Kostas cleared his throat.

"What about Despina Papadopoulos, Uncle Giorgio?"

Uncle Giorgio glared down at him. Then he began to look thoughtful. Hay glanced at Kostas.

"Is she that other girl? The dark-haired one?"

"Yes. The one you called his cousin."

Slowly Uncle Giorgio turned red in the face. All at once he sat down in a chair with a groan.

"Despina! But she's nothing to Stephanos Papadopoulos. Hardly a second cousin. She doesn't even like him! Who does? Still, I made her mad because of Freda. And I may have said some little thing to Despina about the ring . . ."

"Uncle Giorgio!"

"I am the guilty one!" he admitted, facing the fact, as the worry beads burned through his fingers.

"Are you sure it was Despina, Uncle Giorgio?" asked Nicki. "What about Spyros? After all, Stephanos is his *uncle.*"

"Spyros Papadopoulos? Never! Besides, I didn't tell him anything. And besides that, he's home in bed, sick! And tomorrow is Sunday, when I can never be away from the shop for a whole day, even when Spyros is well!"

Uncle Giorgio turned to his elder nephew.

"Nicki, you must lead the way up to the cave tomorrow without me. You must get the ring before Stephanos finds someone to take him there. Because if he goes there he might be lucky and find the ring in its hiding place."

"We will go."

"Can you go tomorrow, Hay?" asked Kostas.

"I hope so," said Hay, but he could have used some worry beads himself at that moment. To ask their parents for permission to go hiking on Mount Parnassus with Uncle Giorgio was one thing. To go without any grown-ups along was another. Their parents would probably have confidence in a full-grown man, but how would they feel about Nicki?

"How far is it?"

"Up and back, it's an all-day trip. It will take more than two hours to get there, especially when you're not used to climbing. It's not scaling up the side of cliffs, but it's hard climbing in a few places."

"If you can go, be here at eight o'clock in the morning," said Nicki, taking command. "We will start then."

Two heads were bent over schoolbooks, but not as industriously as Mrs. Hobbs would probably have liked to see them. It was difficult for Hay and Julia to keep their minds on their studies when they had so much worrying to do.

"I'm sure they won't ever let us go," groaned Julia after a while.

"Be quiet," growled her brother, welcoming the chance to vent some of his ill temper. "I'm trying to do an algebra problem!" He threw down his pencil. "Aw, now you've got me all mixed up."

"I don't care, I'm tired of Norway, and I want to know what we're going to say when they come home and we ask them."

Hay scowled at his pad of scratch paper, and drew a picture of a gibbet, with a man hanging from it by the neck—the man being the Arab who invented algebra. Then all at once his thoughts, as swift-footed as he was slow, swerved into more constructive channels. He jumped up and began to dance about the room.

"I have it!"

"Have what?"

He looked as if he might have any number of things, but at least he looked happy.

"What's the matter with us, Julia? We're forgetting the most important thing!"

"What?"

"The ring! It's not a secret any more about the ring! Stephanos Papadopoulos knows about it, so why shouldn't our own father know about it? We can tell him about the ring now! And when Dad knows we're practically going on an archaeological expedition to recover a real ancient Greek treasure that will end up in the museum, he's *sure* to let us go!"

Julia clapped her hands.

"Maybe you're right! Maybe he'll even want to go, too!" she added, and then grew long-faced again. Hay stopped dancing around, and they looked at each other, thinking over this possible embarrassment. Not that they would have minded too much, but would Nicki want somebody's father to come along? Not likely, he wouldn't! Sighing, Hay sat down again.

79

"Well, we'll have to see about that. Anyway, let's worry about one thing at a time. I think this will work, and that's the important thing."

It worked. Professor Hobbs was all for their going.

"What a great experience for them, I via!" he said to their mother. "Now, I certainly wouldn't want them wandering around up there on their own. I wouldn't even go up there myself without a guide. Nobody's supposed to. But these Greek boys know the mountains, and how to go where they're going, and I'm sure they won't get into any trouble. Anyway, I don't believe in wrapping children in cotton wool as if they were pieces of fragile china. You can't go through life never taking the slightest chance on anything, and be any kind of person. This is the sort of experience they'll never forget! I wish I could go myself, and if Professor Ionides wasn't coming to the museum tomorrow I'm darned if I wouldn't . . ."

The children exchanged a relieved glance and thought pleasant thoughts about Professor Ionides, whoever he might be. Mrs. Hobbs shut her eyes and sighed.

"Well, I suppose I have to have some gray hairs sooner or later, anyway, so why not now?"

ten

When they reached the shop in the morning, Uncle
Giorgio was busy arranging his famous dresses on
their racks for the day. Nicki was helping him.

"Where is Kostas?"

"Looking around," said Uncle Giorgio. "He will
be back soon, and then you can start."

Nicki inspected Hay and Julia, and grinned.
They were wearing sweaters, which felt good in
the chill morning air.

"If the sun stays bright on the mountain, you
will soon take those off."

It seemed more likely to Hay that higher up
on the mountain it would be even chillier. But
before he could go into that, Kostas appeared.

"Well?" said Uncle Giorgio. "Did you find him?"

"No. He's not in the restaurant, and he's not in Dimitri's shop, and Uncle Demos hasn't seen him anywhere this morning."

Uncle Giorgio nodded slowly. He glanced at Hay.

"Stephanos Papadopoulos," he explained. "We would like to know where he is this morning."

Hay was alarmed.

"He won't get to the cave first?"

"I don't think so. I don't think he can find it."

"He didn't fight in the Resistance?"

Uncle Giorgio's lip curled scornfully. "Not Stephanos, not that no-good."

"But he probably knows men who did."

"There was not a man in the Resistance who would take him there, or tell him how to go, not for money or family or anything," Uncle Giorgio declared in a flat, proud tone. "Not even old Achilles would do that, and he's crazy."

"Old who?"

"Old Achilles. He's an old man who lives alone on the mountain, no one knows how. He was a fighter in the mountains, and after the war he was not right in the head. If you should see him, don't bother him, and he won't bother you."

Hay nodded, and then he thought of another possibility.

"What about boys? If Nicki and Kostas know how to go, then maybe some others do, too."

Uncle Giorgio tapped his temple admiringly as he turned to Nicki. "This one, he thinks of everything." But then he shook his head. "No, Hay, I do not think even a boy would help him. But Stephanos is clever, he might learn something from someone who did not know he was telling him anything. So it would be nice to know where he is now, instead of wondering. But go ahead, and keep your eyes open. Just be sure he isn't following you."

Nicki picked up a bulging rucksack that contained their lunch. He slung it on his back, fastened the straps, and looked at his uncle confidently.

"Don't you worry about Stephanos Papado-poulos!"

Two hours later, Hay had learned a lot about mountains. For one thing, he had learned it was possible to climb high up on a mountain and feel hotter than he had ever felt before in his life, even with his sweater long since shed and tied around his waist. He had discovered something about the Greek idea of time, too. Here they were with two hours of hiking already behind them, and it was obvious they still had a long, long way to go. But the heat was the greatest problem of all.

And it was only spring; on some of the peaks in the distance there was still snow; yet perspiration was running down his back as though he had his own Castalia spring in the nape of his neck. The exertion of scrambling up steep stony hillsides and around great rocks in the concentrated sort of sunshine that goes with transparent mountain air in Greece was enough to get anyone steamed up, and Hay was not built for climbing.

He sprawled on the grass of a little meadow, panting, and gazed wonderingly at Nicki and Kostas. It was downright annoying to watch the way they frolicked along. Now they were lolling in the grass, looking cool and comfortable. And Julia, being constructed entirely of steel-spring wires, was having little trouble keeping up. He alone felt as if he were scaling Mount Everest—only a hot Mount Everest instead of a cold one.

Despite his discomfort, however, he was able to look around and feel a vivid sense of elation at being so high in the sky. As unbelievable as it seemed, they were already far above the great cliffs of the Phaidriades. Not that they had climbed them, to be sure! Nobody did that. They had started their ascent up the gentler slope to the west, on the flank of the Shining Ones.

Along the way they had passed shepherds with their flocks of sheep, and old women, dressed in black, taking donkeys up to pasture in the little alpine meadows. Now they could look to the south over the top of Mount Cirphis and see a mountain village where, Kostas said, a festival was held every fall. To the west they could see a massive range of snow-capped peaks, and great sparkling stretches of the Bay of Corinth.

Ahead, grand and remote, towered the summit of Parnassus.

"How much farther is it to the cave?" asked Hay, almost afraid to hear the answer. But Nicki made light of the distance.

"Not far at all now. Just a few more kilometers."

Kilometers! Every kilometer was another six-tenths of a mile. A few of those sounded very far indeed. Fiercely Hay told himself that he was going to stop eating so much and grow thin, very thin, like Julia, so that activities such as hiking would be easier for him; but merely telling himself this reminded him of how ravenously hungry he was that very moment, and made him think about all the good food Nicki was carrying in the rucksack. According to Nicki's plan, they were to have lunch after they had been to the cave and found the ring. If he could only make it that far, at least he would get something to eat!

Nicki stretched and yawned, and then sprang to his feet with a lightness that Hay could only admire without being able to imitate.

"Well, let's move on."

Fighting down a groan, Hay pushed himself up off the grass he had been pressing so comfortably, and took his place in line—third. Nicki first, then Julia, then Hay, then Kostas as their rear guard.

For a long, long time then, it seemed as if they were walking in circles—at least, it would have seemed so had it not been that they kept going up, up, up. Sometimes they picked their way along ledges that were ideal for goats but not so good for a plump boy who could scarcely glance over the edge for fear of getting dizzy. Hay scraped against the rocky face of the slopes the path skirted, and placed his feet carefully on the pebbly trail. Only his good sense of balance gave him any feeling of security. He marveled at the way Nicki and Kostas continued to saunter along as though they were on a path in the public garden in Athens, and consoled himself with the knowledge that they had grown up on those mountain trails.

"Look at the beautiful flower!"

Julia stopped and bent over to inspect a small, brilliant blue blossom that waved on the outer edge of a ledge.

"Julia, stop hanging over the cliff!" snapped Hay, but he could not put much steam into his rebuke. He knew nothing bothered Julia, and that she was as safe hanging over a cliff as she would have been dangling over the edge of a chair.

After a while he even forgot about the occasional scary places, because most of the trek was simply a scramble up endless rocky slopes. His legs ached and he was puffing. He even began to wonder if any ring could be worth all this. But then he reminded himself that it was not just any old ring, but a very special one two or three thousand years old, and that his father was going to be very proud of them for having been part of the expedition that recovered it and brought it down to the museum. Hay's jaw grew firmer in his round cheeks, and he plodded on.

"We're almost there," Nicki said at last. Hay did not know whether to believe him or not. By then he felt as if he were trudging along in a dream that could go on forever and ever. Then something happened that took his mind off his aches and pains. They came up over a slight rise, and there ahead, high above them on a huge shelf of rock, sat a man.

He was a young man, dressed in hiking clothes, with a rucksack by his side much like the one carried by Nicki. On his short blond hair he wore a little green hat ornamented with what looked like a shaving-brush. An Alpine hat, Hay knew it was called, because his father had once considered buying one, but had decided he looked silly in it. The young man also wore a turtle-neck sweater, leather shorts, long woolen socks that reached to his knees, and heavy hiking shoes. He looked down in a wooden-faced way and said, "*Kali mera.*"

"*Kali mera,*" they all replied, in a strained and uneasy way. At such a time, the last thing they wanted to find anywhere near the cave was another human being. Nicki muttered something to Kostas in Greek, over his shoulder, and continued to march ahead. But as they moved on, Hay noticed that Nicki kept darting quick glances back at the man sitting on the ledge.

The first time the path dipped down out of sight, Nicki halted. Without a word Kostas turned aside, crouched low, and began to work his way up to a point on the ridge beside it from which he would be able to see the man they had passed. While they waited silently, watching, Kostas lay on his belly peering through a low screen of brush. Then he edged down again and returned to them quietly.

"He's taken out a bottle of wine, and he's eating bread and cheese, so he won't leave in a hurry."

"Good. But watch him for five minutes to make sure, then catch up with us."

Kostas nodded, and returned to his observation post. The rest of them started on. Ahead, the path moved up a slope again.

"We can't go that way, because he'll see us, and he'll notice three instead of four," Hay pointed out. He knew it might annoy Nicki to be told, if he had not thought of it himself, but this was no time to take chances. And fortunately Nicki was too concerned to be petty. He simply stopped, and nodded.

"We'll go around."

Going around was difficult, but they managed. Not long after they had regained the path, Kostas came padding along behind them, surefooted and tireless.

"It's all right. He's still eating."

They moved on, faster now, anxious. Hay panted miserably and glared at Nicki's straight back. Him and his "almost there"! The momentary excitement of having to cope with the stranger on the ledge faded, and left Hay with only his fatigue and discomfort and hunger again—especially, now, his hunger. Far from alert any more, he was unprepared for the next surprise, except that he noticed the abrupt tensing of Nicki's shoulders an instant before Nicki spoke in a low voice without turning his head.

"Kostas," he all but whispered.

"Yes," said Kostas in the same low voice, and without breaking his stride.

"You saw him."

"Yes. But he doesn't think so."

Nicki made an instant decision.

"We'll stop on the next slope and have lunch."

"He will be able to see us there."

"I want him to."

Once in a long while Julia knew when to keep her mouth shut, and this was one of those times. Instead of asking "Who?" in her clear, high voice, she waited until Nicki stopped and began to undo the straps of his rucksack and told them, "All right, we'll stop here for lunch," loud enough for them all to hear, and for anybody else around to hear if he cared to. Only then did she say it, in a small, quiet voice.

"Who?"

"Stephanos," muttered Nicki as he stooped to set the rucksack on a rock. "Stephanos Papadopoulos."

eleven

Still bent over the rucksack, kneeling beside it now as he took out their food, Nicki continued to explain in a low mutter, while the others clustered around.

"He is behind a big rock above the path fifty meters back. I saw just the corner of his cap."

"So did I," said Kostas, "and one end of his mustache. But it is Stephanos."

"He knows the cave is somewhere near here, and he knew we would come this way. He will watch us and see where we go, and when we stop he will know where the cave is."

"Then what will he do?"

"I don't know, but I know what he is like, and I know he will have a plan." Nicki chuckled excitedly. He was in his element now, playing a game of wits.

91

"But we will have our plan, too. First, we will eat our lunch, and let him wait behind his rock."

For a long time now Hay had been looking forward to food with gluttonous eagerness. But now that lunchtime had unexpectedly materialized, he could not even bring his full powers of concentration to bear on it. He still watched with keen pleasure while Nicki unpacked the rucksack and brought forth sandwiches and black olives, meatballs and *baklava,* and *dolmades*—rice wrapped in grape leaves that had been soaked in olive oil, a Greek specialty that Hay was very fond of. But although he ate his share ravenously, his thoughts failed to center on a voluptuous appreciation of each mouthful of food. His mind was busy with Nicki and Stephanos Papadopoulos, trying to guess what Stephanos might do, and how Nicki planned to outwit him. Nicki sat apart from them, silent, abstracted, his eyes bright with strategic considerations as he slowly munched on a sandwich that scarcely seemed to interest him. Julia and Kostas ate with almost the same preoccupation, glancing now and then at Nicki in much the same way Hay did.

When the last bite of his sandwich was finished, Nicki dusted his fingertips together almost daintily, and took a thermos bottle out of the rucksack.

"Now, while we take turns having a drink of water, we'll talk," he said, motioning them to him. *He ought to be an actor,* Hay thought almost bitterly, for certainly Nicki was acting his part to the hilt and enjoying every moment of it. They gathered

92

in a circle to have a sparing drink of the cold water, and hear a plan.

Once again they were under way along the trail, a trail that twisted and turned, that climbed and dipped, but always climbed more than it dipped. Knowing where the path ran, Stephanos would not find it hard to stay parallel to it, keeping out of sight but still being able to glimpse them frequently. They were under strict orders not to look back, no matter how tempted they were to do so.

They had been walking for ten minutes or so, and were crossing a small ridge that left them exposed to view in every direction, when suddenly Hay's foot slipped. He skidded sideways, and then collapsed on the ground, holding his leg.

"Ooh, my ankle!"

Nicki turned and came back to him, looking disgusted but also alarmed.

"*Now* what's the matter?"

"I twisted my ankle."

Nicki snorted impatiently. "Let me see."

They were all gathered around Hay now as Nicki inspected his ankle. He straightened up and gave Hay an angry tongue-lashing.

"Now you've done it! I knew we shouldn't have let you two come along in the first place! If only Uncle Giorgio had listened to me..."

"It isn't much farther, Nicki," said Kostas.

"That doesn't matter, Hay must start back right away, while he can still walk at all, and you've got to go with him, both of you. We'll be lucky if we don't have to carry him half the way down as it is. I'll go on to the cave, and catch up with you."

They all howled with disappointment, but Nicki was firm.

"Get going, I said! It's not my fault you're so clumsy," he sneered at Hay. He yanked loose the rucksack straps and pulled it off his back. "Here, Kostas, take this with you. No, wait a minute." Nicki rummaged in it before handing it to Kostas. "I'll need the flashlight. Now, get going!"

Flashlight in hand, Nicki turned and strode off up the path, leaving them looking after him.

"Come," said Kostas coldly, and Julia glared at Hay.

"Darn you, anyway!"

"I suppose I did it on purpose!" whined Hay. Wrangling, they plodded off down the path, with Hay limping painfully behind the others. After a while they stopped arguing and walked in silence. For five minutes Hay hobbled along behind, until they reached a point where the path ran below a miniature cliff, a straight-sided slab of rock that rose twenty feet or so above a small thicket of scrubby trees and bushes.

Kostas vanished. One instant he was trudging along the path, the next instant he was gone, with only a slight fluttering of low branches to note his passing. Julia slid in under the trees a split-second behind him. As for Hay, his limp was instantly cured. He too sprang off the trail and wriggled in under the trees with an agility that did him credit.

Nicki had marched them straight past the cave not ten minutes earlier, leading Stephanos on!

Kostas was their leader now, and Kostas was not wasting any time. On hands and knees they followed him through the thicket, with branches whipping their faces and scratching their legs. They did not stop until they had reached the face of the boulder.

Even then it was hard to see the opening. It was naturally camouflaged by a fold in the rock, and perfectly concealed by underbrush and shadows. It appeared to be no more than a dark splotch on the stone, until one looked closer.

Hay watched Kostas open the pack, and wished he could have said what he was thinking, but they had agreed not to talk. He was thinking, *that was the best part, the rucksack part, that was Nicki's best idea.* To make sure Stephanos would be fooled into following him, Nicki had taken his flashlight before he handed the rucksack over to Kostas. But that had been only half the trick. Because the big problem for the rest of them, the other three of them, had been how could *they* carry a flashlight? None of them had a pocket large enough to hold one, let alone any way of concealing one; and if Stephanos had seen *them* take a flashlight, he would have become suspicious at once. So Nicki had taken his and given the rucksack to Kostas to carry back. Who would stop to think that the pack might have *two* flashlights in it?

Kostas pulled out the second one now, grinned his

face-splitting grin at them, and jerked his head at the cave opening. They followed him inside, crouching on hands and knees, and then, almost at once, wriggling on their stomachs in a breathless, pebble-scraping blackness. Once they were fairly through the opening, the tunnel entrance turned abruptly to the right and slanted slightly downward. Hay ducked his head as Julia's sneakers kicked pebbles in his face, and marveled dreamily at the fact that there was not even time to get scared. A few feet more in the utter darkness, and he was startled by the unearthly, hollow sound of Kostas whispering to Julia, "You can stand up now." Hay edged forward, and nearly jumped out of his skin as a hand touched him.

"Stand up," said Kostas.

There is no other darkness like the darkness of a cave. The blackness muffled Hay like a garment and was so thick he felt sure it must be solid, and that he would bump his head hard if he raised it. But he obeyed Kostas and found there was headroom. He could scarcely sense that the others were there, even though he knew they were.

"Now," said Kostas, and switched on the flashlight.

No feat of magic had ever amazed them more than did that simple act. They gasped when the rocky interior of the cave sprang into existence around them. Flecks of quartz crystal winked at them, preventing the walls from seeming as dark and grim and dead as Hay had expected. The surfaces were rough and uneven, and arched together at a height of nine or ten feet in the center, leaving an open space below them no larger than Hay's bedroom at home. Even so, quite a few men could have been inside the chamber. It was a bloodtingling thought to know that guerrilla fighters had hidden there, right where they were standing. How many men had cleaned their rifles and checked their precious ammunition while sitting with their backs against these very stones, a score of years ago, long before he or Julia or Kostas were even born? All that was history now, too, as much as were all the stories about the ancient Greeks.

Even though they were inside, Kostas spoke in the most cautious of whispers. It was hard to imagine conversing in a normal voice in such a place at any time.

"There is another room!"

"Another one? Where?"

"Here!"

Again there was an opening that would have escaped notice unless a person looked hard. A rugged fold in the one rocky wall kept it out of sight from the center of the chamber. Kostas stooped down and flashed his light through the oblique aperture. Gathered behind him, peering over his shoulder, Hay and Julia could see into the second room.

"The ring is in there."

One after another they crawled through and stood up in a space nearly as long as the first chamber but much narrower. As the circle of light traveled around the walls, it revealed nothing but bare, glistening rock. It was hard to see how those flat surfaces could possibly provide a hiding place for anything, even something so small as a gold ring.

Kostas uttered a single, worried syllable.

"Oh!"

"What's the matter?"

"We need Nicki. It's high on the wall, higher than we can reach!"

They stared at each other. Then Hay put his back against the wall and knit his fingers together, ready to give Kostas a leg up. Kostas nodded, and handed Julia the flashlight.

"Good. There is a little place high up . . ."

"A ledge?"

"You call it that? Yes, very small, and on the right side, here."

They made several tries, Hay grunting as Kostas stepped into his hands and balanced above him, groping high over his own head along the hard surfaces of what looked like an unbroken expanse of bare rock.

"More," said Kostas, and Hay struggled to lift him higher, while the Greek boy's toe dug cruelly into his stomach. Kostas' straining fingers scrabbled along the rock, and the same thought began to gnaw at them all. What if, after all this, the ring was not there? What if someone else had already found it, perhaps long ago?

Kostas stepped down again, and he and Hay stood panting at each other, gasping both from exertion and from near-despair.

Then Kostas had *his* great moment. It was Kostas who had thought about the dark-haired girl Despina

Papadopoulos and made Uncle Giorgio realize that it was he himself who had given away the secret of the ring. And it was Kostas now who remembered something very important.

"Uncle Petros!" he exclaimed, and his face lit up. "I have seen many pictures of him, and now I remember something. He is not tall. In fact, Uncle Petros is very short!"

Hay's own face began to clear as he pounced on the logical conclusion Kostas was getting at.

"So when Uncle Petros says the little ledge is high up on the wall, what he thinks of as high isn't really very high at all!"

Hay all but sprang back to the wall, and Kostas was stepping into his hands the instant he was ready. Three more times they tried, moving along the rocky sides of the cave, and the third time was the charm. Kostas let out a sharp glad cry that hurt their ears as it bounced off the close stone walls. He stepped down with a small sack in his hand.

"A tobacco sack!" said Hay.

"Yes, but there's something hard in it," said Kostas, working the drawstring top open. While Julia held the flashlight beam on it he tipped the sack over his palm, and a mellow wheel of fire rolled out. A flat circle of gold glowed against his olive skin. Kostas stood with twenty-five centuries in the palm of his hand. Nobody said anything. Time stood still while they looked.

"I never saw anything so beautiful," said Julia finally.

"My father . . ." began Hay, and couldn't think of anything more to say. But Julia glanced at him with a face that was glowing like the ring, and he knew she understood what he meant.

It was Kostas who remembered first, remembered where they were and what they still had to do. He dropped the ring back into the bag, closed it, and put it in his pocket.

"Come!"

Two minutes later they were crouched in the thicket again while Kostas' keen eyes made sure no one was near, and already the cave seemed like a part of a dream as they blinked out at sunlight.

Kostas strapped on the rucksack again.

"All right," he said, and one after another they shot out of the thicket back onto the trail, picking up their single-file march as if they had never stopped. And now they were laughing with relief, because the worst was over and the best was ahead. Soon Nicki would come running down the path behind them, and everything would be perfect—Stephanos Papadopoulos outwitted, and the ring found. Kostas was not worried about Stephanos now, he said, because even Stephanos would not dare take the ring away from them by force. Whatever Stephanos' plan was, it was not that, Kostas said. He would not dare.

He was saying this when, somewhere in the distance behind them, they heard two sharp, vicious reports crack and reverberate among the stony peaks and chasms of Mount Parnassus. Kostas stopped in his tracks. When his head snapped around his face was pale.

"Those were shots," he said. "Gun shots!"

twelve

The reverberation of the shots seemed to go on forever. Hay's cheeks grew cold as the blood left them. He felt dizzy, and sick. There was only one person or thing on Mount Parnassus that anybody might be shooting at, as far as they were concerned.

Kostas reacted unthinkingly, and with the courage they might have expected. He simply turned, his face set and pale, and began to run back in the direction the shots had come from. And Hay and Julia followed him just as unthinkingly. Not even Hay had any clear idea in mind as to exactly what they could do when they reached wherever Nicki was, but all of them knew they could not bear just to stand and wait and wonder. It was grotesque and unbelievable to think that anything horrible had actually happened to Nicki, but they had to know.

Their headlong race back up the path was a nightmarish scramble, and one in which Kostas soon left the others behind. In a minute or two he was out of sight. With lungs seemingly ready to burst, Hay stumbled to a stop and called to Julia, who was well ahead of him, but far behind Kostas.

"Wait!"

She hesitated, looked back, and came to a reluctant halt, impatient to go on. Hay hated himself for being so fat and slow, but he could not push himself along any faster, and he did not want Julia to run ahead alone.

"Slow down," he panted. "We can't keep up with Kostas, anyway."

"What can we do?" Julia was close to tears.

"I don't know. We have to find out what has happened first, and maybe you'll be the one who will have to go for help. Save something for that. Let's keep going, but not run."

Even just to keep going was not easy, but Hay struggled on. Then suddenly, unexpectedly, the ordeal was finished. Over a rise ahead of them, a sunburst of glory with a broad grin of triumph on his face, came Nicki, with Kostas trotting beside him. Hay and Julia skidded to a stop and stared openmouthed.

"Turn around! Why are you running this way, just because of a few shots?" asked Nicki in a cocky, teasing tone. He laughed delightedly. "That Stephanos! He had a good plan, all right. Some day I will even tell him so! Come on, I'll tell you about it while we walk," he said, passing them and taking the lead.

"Okay, okay! Go on!" cried Hay, in a fever of impatience.

"Well . . . After a few minutes of walking I stopped and began to look around. Then, still looking around like this," said Nicki, glancing about him furtively, acting again, "I went toward an opening in some rocks. Bang! bang! Stephanos shot twice over my head from behind some little bushes beside a rock, and in a strange voice he called out, 'Get away from my cave! Go away, or I'll shoot you!' "

Kostas doubled over with laughter.

"He was pretending to be Old Achilles!"

"That's right," said Nicki. "Old Achilles has never bothered anybody, but still, he might sometime. So that was Stephanos' plan. After we had showed him where the cave was, he planned to scare us away before we could go into it, by making us think the old man had really gone mad."

"Only there wasn't any cave," said Hay.

Nicki gave him his foxy look. "Oh, yes, there was! There really is a cave up there, too—another one that I knew about—and right now Stephanos Papadopoulos is in it, looking everywhere!"

It was good to laugh again. In fact, they began to laugh so hard they had to stop for a minute. And while they were stopped, Kostas took out the little sack and showed Nicki the ring.

"Isn't it beautiful?" said Julia. Nicki's face grew serious, almost tender, as he looked at it.

"Yes. It must be worth a lot of money," he said.

"You carry it, Nicki," said Kostas, and Nicki put it in his pocket.

"I'll take the rucksack now, too."

"You don't have to. It's very light."

"All right, carry it if you want to. Turn around." While Kostas stood still like a pack-horse, Nicki put his flashlight back inside the rucksack and fastened the straps again. "Now! Let's go home!"

During the next bone-wrenching couple of hours, Hay learned something else about mountains. He learned that going down was almost harder work than going up. Only the exhilaration of their triumph carried him through. As he slipped and slid and scrambled down one rocky slope after another, each step seemed enough to jolt his teeth out of his head, and his private Castalia spring was a torrent again down his back.

They made short stops from time to time, and shared what little water was left. When it was gone, and they were all very thirsty, Julia saved the day. To Hay's surprise, she produced a package of chewing gum and offered each of them a stick.

"Thanks, Julia," said Hay, almost awe-stricken. He knew how little was left of her precious store, and how jealously she guarded it. Probably she had been struggling with herself all this time, trying to decide whether or not to be generous. And finally her better self had won out. Sharing this prized possession was a real sacrifice on her part. And never could she have chosen a time when it helped more.

They started the final leg of their descent in high spirits. Hay and Julia laughed at the way Nicki chewed his gum—he looked as if he were snapping at it with his strong white teeth—and Julia showed them how she could make it pop, even though it was not the bubble variety.

Once more Hay's mind was full of thoughts of how pleased their father would be, and how excited. Hay could hardly wait to have him see the ring.

"Nicki, I wonder . . . could we go by the museum on our way?"

He knew it wasn't really on their way, but that they could cut over above the town to the sanctuary if Nicki was willing. Nicki glanced back at him agreeably.

"To show your father, I suppose?"

"Yes!"

Nicki shrugged.

"Why not? Then we'll go on to the shop and give it to Uncle Giorgio."

"That's great, Nicki! Thanks!"

They followed a trail that would bring them around the far end of the stadium, and familiar landmarks began to appear. Even some tourists were in sight now, strolling along the paths. Ten minutes more, and they would be in the museum!

Instead of following the walk that zigzagged sedately through the sanctuary, Nicki led them to a shortcut which dropped to a lower path alongside a large boulder. And as they scrambled down single file, Hay had the pleasure of seeing Nicki's foot slip for once, and of watching him slide the last yard or two on the seat of his pants, right to the feet of a man who strode into sight at that instant from behind the boulder, wearing a turtleneck sweater and a hat with a shaving-brush.

The hiker!

The man pulled up short, looked at Nicki in his wooden-faced way, and then reached down and helped him to his feet. Hay was so surprised to see the man again that he had to grab a branch to keep from sliding after Nicki.

"*Efharistó!*" Nicki thanked him, as he got to his feet.

"*Parakaló,*" replied the hiker. A brief nod, and he was gone, striding away in his businesslike way. The children gathered around Nicki while he dusted off the seat of his shorts. They stared after the hiker in amazement.

"Well, what do you know?" said Hay. "Him again!"

"I was so surprised I almost swallowed my gum," said Nicki, chewing fiercely. "What is it you say? It's a small world?"

"That's right!"

"Well, come on, let's go."

They stayed on the path now, and watched the hiker walk on down to the highway, cross it, and get into a small car. By then they had nearly reached the museum themselves.

"Well, that's the last of *him*," said Hay. "Now, if

only Dad is here. . . ."

Nicki led the way to the museum entrance, but there Hay had to take over. The guard at the door knew he and Julia were Professor Hobbs's children. When Hay explained that they wanted to see his father, the guard let them all come in without buying tickets.

"Where will he be, Hay?"

"Probably upstairs in the room where they're working on new exhibits. It's closed off, but we can get in."

It was such a fine afternoon that most of the tourists were outside, enjoying the sunshine. Only a few were in the museum. The children hurried upstairs and through two exhibition rooms to the door Hay had in mind. But when he knocked there was no answer. He put his ear to the door, and heard no sound of anyone inside. They asked a guard if he had seen the professor, and were told he had not.

"I'll go down and find out if any of the other museum people know where he is," said Hay, and puffed away downstairs again, with Julia tagging along at his heels. There they found a member of the museum staff, who told them their father had gone out with Professor Ionides and that they were somewhere in the sanctuary.

Hay and Julia exchanged a disappointed glance.

"Well, we can't ask Nicki and Kostas to traipse all over the sanctuary looking for him now. I guess we'll have to go on."

They went upstairs again to tell Nicki, and found

Kostas near the room the Naxian Sphinx was in.

"Your father's not in any of these rooms," he said. "Nicki is looking in the other ones."

Hay was telling Kostas their news when suddenly Nicki came rushing toward them with a wild look.

"Come on!" he cried, beckoning sharply as he hurried past them. There was not even time to ask him what was the matter, but disaster was written all over his face.

A place like the Delphi Museum is not one in which it is proper for boys and girls to fly down the stairs like a bunch of rowdies, but they came close to it as they followed him, and drew a frown from the guard at the door as they swirled through it.

Outside Nicki raced toward the road, and then skidded to a stop.

"He's gone!"

"Who?"

"That hiker!" Nicki whirled and slapped his pocket. "He picked my pocket! He took the ring! It's gone!"

thirteen

Hearing the words was like getting kicked in the stomach. Julia seemed to wilt like a flower. She sat down on a low wall that bordered the walk, and gulped hard. Kostas dropped down beside her and brushed a hand across his burning eyes. Hay caught his breath, and asked, "Are you sure, Nicki?"

Nicki turned his pockets inside out, both of them. They were empty.

"But—but that man just happened—"

"He didn't just *happen* to be there," snapped Nicki. "He must have been watching us all the time, and looking for a chance to get near us. Maybe Stephanos was stupid, but he wasn't as stupid as I thought!"

"You think they were working together?"

"Of course! They *must* have been!"

Hay still looked for some ray of hope—anything.

"Maybe it just slipped out of your pocket when you fell."

"I don't think so, but let's go look, anyway."

A moment earlier it would not have seemed possible to Hay that he could have run another step up a steep path, but now he found himself doing it. When they reached the place by the big boulder where Nicki had slipped, they searched the ground inch by inch. But they found no small tobacco sack anywhere.

"I told you it wouldn't be here."

"Maybe someone came along and found it."

"Not many people are walking this way now. And if somebody *did* find it . . ." Nicki made a cynical whistling sound and waved his hand to show it would be gone forever.

"Someone might turn it in."

"Who would do that?" he said scornfully.

"Well, we can hope," said Hay, but he could not put much confidence into his tone of voice.

"We might as well go tell Uncle Giorgio. Come on."

They retreated down the path like a beaten army, silent, bowed, and bitter. And Hay, his head down and his mind recovering from mere turmoil, was beginning to grapple with a new and uncomfortable line of thought.

"You go ahead," he said, when they had reached the museum again. "We might as well wait here till Dad comes back."

"I don't blame you," said Nicki, misreading Hay's mind. "I don't look forward to seeing Uncle Giorgio."

They watched Nicki and Kostas trudge off along the walk beside the highway, and then sat down on the wall outside the museum. Julia was too depressed even to talk, so that Hay was able to think in peace and quiet. And he had plenty to think about.

After a long time he groaned like someone in great pain, and turned to his sister.

"Julia, do you believe that man picked Nicki's pocket and took the ring?"

She stared at him wide-eyed.

"Well, of course! It was gone, wasn't it?"

Hay continued to stare back at her, silently, relentlessly, until she gasped

"You mean, you don't believe he did?"

"No," he said sadly, "I don't believe he did."

"Hay!"

"Well, I don't."

"Well, if he didn't, what happened to it?"

"I think Nicki made up the story."

"What!"

"Well, don't tell *me* he wouldn't have felt in his pocket to see if it was still there, after he fell down! If it had been me carrying it, I would have been checking my pocket every other step of the way down to make sure it was still safe!"

"Nicki's different."

"Not *that* different. So how come he didn't notice it was missing until *after* we got to the museum, and *after* he could be pretty sure that man had already driven away?"

Julia gaped at him, and her silence made it plain that he was beginning to shake her own confidence in Nicki's story.

"I think he still had the ring when we got to the museum, and only pretended he had lost it," Hay went on. "That means he hid it somewhere in the museum. But where? Where could he put it in there? He had to hide it some place where it would be safe, where nobody else would happen to notice it until he could come back and get it. And where could that be? Where could that be in a museum where hundreds of people come every day, and any one of them might look behind or under or on top of anything that's in the museum?"

Julia's reaction was a funny contradiction. She shook her head helplessly, but at the same time she sprang to her feet and said, "Let's go look!"

When they reached the second floor of the museum, Hay muttered, "Remember what Kostas said? He said Nicki was looking for Dad in the other rooms. He meant the ones at the other end, on the side opposite where we were. So that's where we have to look for the ring."

Just as he had feared, their search seemed hopeless. The exhibition rooms, with their marble statues and funeral steles, their fragments of pediments and their capitals from columns, seemed to offer no possible hiding place for anything, however small. Hay began to wonder if he was being unfair to Nicki, if his theory was a nasty one he would later be ashamed of, but he could not believe it. He could not shake off the feeling that something was wrong with Nicki's story, that something about Nicki's actions had not quite rung true, just as Nicki did not quite ring true in anything he did. Nicki the actor. As a matter of

115

fact, somehow Nicki had not even *looked* quite right, though for the life of him Hay could not figure out just what it was about the way Nicki had appeared that had bothered him. What had changed? *Something* had, but he could not think what it was.

One room after another yielded nothing in the way of a hiding place where anything could be concealed with any sense of security—not a niche, not a crack, not a slit behind anything, not a high place on top of anything. The end room was the most discouraging of all, since it contained only two display cases against the wall, and the bronze statue of the Charioteer standing straight and tall in the center. Slowly, dejectedly, they walked around the statue, circling the room and looking without hope into its wide-open corners. Two tourists who had been studying the Charioteer glanced at their wrist watches, said something to each other about their bus, and left. Hay and Julia were alone.

"How could anyone hide anything in here?" she sighed.

And almost before she had finished speaking, they stopped at the same instant, staring at the back of the Charioteer. They had forgotten something important about him.

Being a statue cast in bronze, he was hollow. Furthermore, he had been found in two parts, and at the small of his back, where the two pieces of his body fitted together, there was a hole in him. A roughly oval hole, about large enough for a hand to go through comfortably.

"Hay! Maybe . . ."

But Hay was already shaking his head.

"That's silly. If Nicki dropped the bag inside the Charioteer, how could he ever get it out again?"

Julia thought hard, hating to give up the idea.

"With a magnet?" she said uncertainly.

"A magnet? Don't be dumb! A magnet can't attract *gold!*"

"Oh."

"Only iron."

"Oh."

"And anyway, look how far down inside it would be! Look how tall he is!"

"I know, but . . . Oh, I wish we could find it!"

"So do I, but crazy ideas won't help any," grumbled Hay. He was in a thoroughly bad mood by now, because his detective's mind was leading him nowhere.

"Maybe the man really did take it, Hay."

He sighed heavily.

"Maybe he did."

They walked gloomily back through the museum. Nobody else was in sight. They were all alone in a dead world, and Hay had never felt more depressed.

"I guess we'll never know. And that's what I hate most of all—always having to wonder!"

There were times when sisters, even sisters like Julia, could be understanding. This was one of those times. After no more than a momentary struggle with herself, Julia offered what consolation she could. Producing the remains of her special treat, she tore the last stick of gum in two, being careful to make the pieces even.

"Here. You can have half," she said. But when she looked up, Hay was gone.

fourteen

For the next few minutes it was all Julia could do to keep up with Hay for once. First she followed him through the museum, and then she trailed him down the stairs and outside. He was burning with indignation. He was going to march straight to the shop and tell Uncle Giorgio everything.

But the further they went, the more he slowed down. He was thinking about Kostas, and the more he thought about Kostas the heavier their new secret became.

"I hate to think how Kostas is going to feel," he muttered.

"So do I," said Julia so quickly that he knew she had been thinking about him, too. "And Uncle Giorgio. They'll be so ashamed they'll want to die."

"They think Nicki is the greatest thing around," Hay added bitterly.

"What are we going to do?"

"We *have* to tell them. We can't let him get away with it," said Hay, but nevertheless he continued to slow down. Soon he stopped altogether and sagged onto the low parapet that ran alongside the road. Sitting like a lump on the hard stones, he stared out across the Sea of Olives, and his eyes glittered with misery. Julia stood on one foot and then the other, and finally sat beside him, her hands clenched in her lap. Hay frowned darkly.

"You know what, Julia? I wish we didn't know!"

He loved nothing better than to figure out puzzles about people, and he had never solved a better one. But this time the fun was missing. Now he was left with a problem that *had* no good solution.

"If we tell, it's bad, and if we don't, it's bad . . ."

He paused. Julia had jumped up and was pointing.

"What's the matter?"

"Hay! Look!"

From the direction of the town, around the bend in the road, two figures had appeared.

"It's Nicki and Kostas!"

Hay stared, jolted by the sight.

"Why are they coming back? *Both* of them," he added, and dismissed a horrible suspicion as soon as it occurred to him. No! Kostas *couldn't* be part of it. But why was he with his cousin? Why—if Nicki was returning so soon at all—why wasn't Nicki sneaking back to the museum alone?

The Greek boys seemed as shocked to see Hay and Julia as they were to see them. Nicki and Kostas exchanged nervous glances and a few quick words, and looked so guilty that Hay's heart sank. Even Kostas looked uneasy! Hay stood up, waiting for them.

"Hello. Where are you going?"

The boys stopped, and exchanged another glance. Kostas' eyes and cheeks looked smeary, as though they had been wet.

"Tell them," said Kostas. "You must tell them, because they will have to know anyway."

Nicki's face was already red. Now it became more so. He scowled at the ground.

"Oh, all right!" He looked up at Hay. "I hid the ring in the museum. It was only a trick. I thought of the whole plan in a flash, just like that," he said, snapping his fingers with sudden irrepressible pride in his own cleverness. "I was looking for your father, and I thought, 'Why should we give the ring away for nothing, when it could be sold for a lot of money?' And I thought of everything, the whole plan, all at once! I could hide the ring and say that the man who bumped into me took it. And at the same time I thought of how to hide it, because I was behind the Charioteer, and he has a hole in him. Do you know what I did? I took my chewing-gum and stuck it on the strings of the bag, and stuck the bag on the inside of the Charioteer!"

Hay was trembling so that he could not even speak. Nicki obviously thought he was speechless from surprise.

"It was such a good trick to think of all at once that I did it—pouf!—just like that. I *had* to try it, it was so good. I did it on an impulse, the way I always do things when I think of them. Well, then we started back to the shop, and I wished I hadn't done it, but now it was too late."

"But Uncle Giorgio wasn't there," said Kostas. "I am so glad he wasn't there!"

"Spyros Papadopoulos is feeling better, and he is taking care of the shop. Uncle Giorgio was getting worried about us, so he had gone up on Agia Ilias to meet us!"

Nicki paused and glanced at Kostas with a strange look on his face, half angry and half ashamed.

"We waited around outside, wondering what to do. Then Kostas began to cry. Kostas, who never cries! You could twist his arm till it broke, he wouldn't cry, but now he was crying. I asked him why. He said he was ashamed we had lost the ring. He said it would disgrace our whole family! Well, that is foolish! But I couldn't stand to see the little idiot cry, so we will get the ring back. I was going to, anyway . . . at least, I think I was," added Nicki, with impulsive honesty. "It was one of those things I do all of a sudden, because I think of them and want to try."

As Hay listened, he felt relief and regret, and both gladness and sorrow, but most of all he felt compassion. Nicki was like no one else he had ever met. Cleverness was his great talent, but it was also his fatal flaw. Where would it lead him? Even now,

Nicki was only half convinced that what he had done was wrong. Kostas had forgiven him, because he had confessed and was on his way to set things straight. But would Kostas ever feel quite the same about his clever cousin again?

What Hay might have said at that moment he never knew, because before he could think of what he wanted to say, Kostas' gasp took all their attention.

"Look! Here comes Uncle Giorgio!"

Uncle Giorgio must have walked down to the museum, because he was coming from that direction. Perhaps he had met someone on the path above the sanctuary who had seen them come that way. In any event, he was approaching them, and Nicki's face became as pale as it had been red. Here was sudden disaster, when he had least expected it.

"Quick, before he—"

But it was too late. Uncle Giorgio already had seen them, and was waving. Nicki looked around wildly, but he was trapped. He could not run away now, he could not quietly disappear after one of his tricks.

"What can I tell him? What can I say?" His voice broke. "Now he will have to know my shame!"

Hay reached into his pocket. He held out his hand to Nicki.

"Here."

Nicki stared. His knees all but buckled under him.

"You—you *found* it?"

"Something about you didn't look right when you said the ring was gone, and I finally remembered

what it was. You weren't chewing gum any more!"

Nicki took the precious bag and sat down on the parapet, overwhelmed. He looked ready to burst into tears, but after a struggle he managed to grin. He glanced up at Hay.

"I'll never be a crook, never! I might meet a policeman as smart as you!"

Hay's chest swelled as though Nicki had pinned a medal on it. For Nicki to say such a thing was the greatest tribute he could have been paid.

Uncle Giorgio was near enough now to call to them.

"Well? Did you find it?"

Nicki stood up, and at first Hay thought he was going to run to his uncle with the ring. But maybe Nicki was growing up after all. He looked down at his cousin, and respect and affection were in his eyes. He held out the little bag.

"Here," he said gruffly. "You take it."

Kostas was thunderstruck. For such an honor to be his! He held out his hand hesitantly, as if he were afraid it could not be true. Then his special grin split his face from ear to ear. He whirled around, holding the prize high in the air, and raced toward his uncle.

"Uncle Giorgio! We have the ring!"